The Heart
of
A Lion

by

Ronna M. Bacon

Jeremiah 29:11

11 For I know the thoughts that I think toward you, says the Lord, thoughts of peace and not of evil, to give you a future and a hope.

Table of Contents

Prologue

The young boy stood and watched as his father was handcuffed and led away by the police. He couldn't understand why. His mother didn't come from the kitchen when he called for her. The woman police officer standing beside him led him away from his home. He kicked at her and screamed that he didn't want to go, but she kept a strong grip on his arm and still took him away from his home and his mother. He was put into the back of her cruiser, tears pouring down his face. What had happened? Why didn't his mother answer him?

The veteran police officers cleared the scene, watching the young boy through the windows. They knew why his mother wasn't answering him and why his father didn't come. They had seen too many of these calls over the years.

His attention turning to the officers, the young boy's heart began to harden. It was their fault, he decided, their fault, all of them. And when he grew up, they would all pay for keeping him from his mother and taking his father away.

Chapter 1

Doug Foster pulled the door to his Uncle Mac's cafe open and stepped inside, relishing the warmth after the dampness and coldness of the late summer day. He shook off the raindrops from his jacket and headed for the counter, where only one empty stool remained. He seated himself, waved at Mac, then spun to survey the cafe. It was full, normal for it at noon. He raised a hand in greeting to friends, then turned as someone spoke to him.

"Doug, stop ignoring us."

Dave Allison, senior paramedic in their hometown of Riverville and a good friend, was grinning at him from the other side of a woman. Doug acknowledged him, then his gaze stopped.

"Darcy? Darcy O'Shaughnessy?" His voice was full of wonder and delight. "You're here in my town?"

The auburn-haired woman turned her hazel eyes to Doug. "Doug Foster! This is your town? I never knew."

He studied her face and nodded. More than likely she had forgotten. It had been years since they had been friends in college.

"It's so great to see you." He turned as Mac set his meal down in front of him. "Thanks, Mac."

Darcy looked in wonder as the meal appeared without Doug ordering. "How'd he do that? You never ordered."

Doug shook his head. "No, I never have to. And once you've ordered here, unless you tell Mac differently, you'll get the same order every time. I don't know how he does it but he remembers what you want. Besides, he's my uncle and has heard my opinions of food for many years."

Dave snorted from the other side of Darcy. "And we've all heard your opinions at one time or another."

"Shut up, Dave." Doug's attention turned from his meal to the TV playing silently overhead. His hand dropped his fork back to the plate as he watched, shocked at the images and the newsfeed running in front of his eyes. He was up and out the door before Dave or Darcy could even ask what was wrong.

Darcy stared at the door he had disappeared through, then turned to Dave. "What happened?"

Dave nodded at the TV. "That. Doug's the lieutenant in charge of our police emergency task force or response team as some call them. They'll be on call to help over in Greentown."

Darcy felt shell-shocked as she looked at the TV. Who had done this?

Doug entered the conference room that was always set aside for the ETF men. He found his men gathered, all in from their day off, grim and stern looks on their faces as they followed the news report showing pictures of the scene, emergency vehicles parked haphazardly with their lights flashing, emergency personnel standing or wandering around almost aimlessly. Yellow caution tape spanned a large area around a low-rise apartment building. News teams vied for the attention of those officers who appeared to be in charge. Bystanders stood, some still in their nightclothes, rushed from the building for their safety. The rainy, dark day only added to the unreal aspect of the scene.

"Tom, what do we know so far?"

Tom Allison, Dave's brother and second-in-command to their team, turned. "It's not good, Doug. The ETF in Greentown answered a hostage call real early, about 3 a.m. at that apartment building and were ambushed. In the melee that followed, bystanders were killed and hurt. They've lost some men as well from the team."

Sorrow etched its way onto Doug's face. "Have we been called yet?"

"No. They did ask us to be on standby in case they need us. The call went out to all the ETFs in the area."

"Any word on who yet?"

Tom shook his head. "Not yet. If there is, they're not saying. I'm sure we'll hear soon." He looked around the room. "Our guys are taking this hard."

Doug nodded, then turned to leave. "I'll be in my office or with Caleb. Come find me if you hear anything."

Doug exited, almost running into Riverville Police Chief Caleb Logan. Caleb's face was set in stern lines and he motioned for Doug to follow him. Once settled into Caleb's office, Doug spoke.

"You've heard from the chief over there?"

Caleb nodded. "I have. They're keeping as much out of the media as is possible so far. He did share with me that it was a total setup, that there was no hostage. They were targeted, Doug, and they're working through that. That's going to take a while, I suspect."

Doug agreed. "If it's like here, it will. I am at a loss for words to know what to say." He looked down at his hands, then back at Caleb, not only the chief but a close personal friend. "This is when our faith takes us through, these difficult times."

"That it does." Caleb stopped speaking, then continued, "He did say they lost three men, two others are in critical condition.	There were four bystanders killed. Whoever planned this didn't care for the casualties that would happen."

Doug stood to leave. "No, they didn't. I don't like this, Caleb.	Is this just the beginning of a reign of terror against us or is this an isolated incident?"

Caleb shook his head. "We don't have enough information yet, Doug.	Let me know if you get called out over there."

"I will." Doug stood for a minute in the corridor, then headed for his office. He needed to pull paperwork on his men to see who would be around and who had time off booked. He had a gut feeling that this was not over and his feelings like this were usually right.

A tap at his door a couple of hours later raised his head from the paperwork. Dave stood there.

"How are you, Doug?"

Doug shrugged. "In shock, I think. Worried about our guys."

Dave slowly sank into the chair across from him. "Do you think it will affect us or happen here?"

"Who knows?" Doug's eyes strayed past Dave to the wall behind him. "It's entirely possible. I pray not, but I have to be prepared. On another note, how'd you meet Darcy?"

"Darcy? She's moved to town to set up a shop downtown, near the cafe. She's focusing on local artisans, hoping to showcase their crafts to the tourists. She saw Mom's quilts at the last show they had and approached her about showcasing some of them." His eyes narrowed. "How do you know her?"

"College. That seems so far away." Doug was lost in thought, not seeing the speculative glance Dave shot him before nodding his head.

She was the one, Dave thought. She was the one Doug was interested in, then walked away from when he settled on his career.

Dave looked up as Tom knocked at Doug's door and then entered.

"What's the word, Tom?" Doug didn't like the look on his face.

Tom shook his head, unable to find words to speak. Finally, he said, voice raspy with emotion, "They were targeted, Doug, just like it was thought. They found notes at the scene." He stopped, staring ahead at nothing, then bringing his eyes back to Doug. "I just got off the phone with the Greentown police chief. Every ETF team in the area has been targeted. Whoever it is wants to take all of us down."

Doug sat back, shock coursing through his body. "Every team?"

Tom nodded. "So how do we protect one another? This guy is sick." He paused, then continued, "And it's not just the police he's after. He has threatened the fire departments, EMS, social services. I don't know if there's a profession he didn't touch in his notes."

Dave looked down at his phone as a text message came in. "Looks as if words getting out. We all just got called in for an emergency meeting. Stay safe, guys, and don't forget to pray. God's still in control."

Chapter 2

Darcy looked around her shop. It was finally coming together. It had taken a lot of work, contacting the local artisans, but there was such a variety of items offered. She prayed that the store would take off and that the artisans would benefit from it. There wasn't another store like hers in town, and she wondered at that.

She stepped outside to study the window display, inadvertently bumping a passerby.

He stopped and glared at her, immediately yelling at her.

She moved away from him, but he followed her across the sidewalk as she moved towards the road. She apologized, but it was if the man hadn't heard a word she said. She could feel the fear starting to rise within her. No, Lord, not now. Not a panic attack. Not in the street and in front of the bystanders. And by the way, Lord, why isn't someone coming to my aid?

She heard a vehicle stop behind her and felt a presence near her. As the man reached for her arm, a hand flew out and grabbed his wrist, at the same time an arm swept her off to the side and behind her rescuer. She watched as the man was thrust against a car and then handcuffed. A patrol officer was there to arrest him and take him away.

She felts hands on her arms and then she was led back into her store and the door closed and locked, the open sign turned to closed. She was shoved down into a chair.

She looked up in protest, words dying on her lips as she saw who it was. Doug! How had he gotten there so fast?

"Are you all right?" Doug's voice faintly penetrated the fog she was in. When she didn't answer, he crouched down in front of her. "Darcy, are you all right?"

She was finally able to nod. He stood, headed for the back, and was back with a bottle of water. "I didn't see any cups, but drink."

She shook her head, but he took the bottle, twisted off the cap, and thrust it back

into her hands. "Drink, or I'll make you."
His deep blue eyes held concern for her.

She finally took a sip, then reached for
the cap. "I'm okay, Doug. Really. I am."

He shook his head. "You could have
fooled me, Darcy. What happened?"

She shook her head, worry pooling in
her eyes. "I don't know. I went outside to
check the window display and somehow
bumped into him. That started off the tirade.
It shouldn't have escalated that way." She
looked at him. "Who was he?"

"The patrol officer will find out for
me. He'll be charged at the very least with
causing a public disturbance, and from the
alcohol I could smell, being intoxicated in a
public place. That's not our town, Darcy.
We have very few incidents of this kind.
Other kinds, yeah, we do."

"What other kinds?" She narrowed
her eyes as he shook his head. "Not telling
me something again, Doug? Is that how it
will be every time we meet, and we speak?
Not really talking about what's going on?
You did that before, Doug, and then just

walked away." She stood and brushed past him, heading for the back room.

Doug reached and stopped her, leaving his hand on her upper arm. He had forgotten her temper, that could flare at him with good reason. And she was right. Today, he wasn't thinking straight.

"I'm sorry, Darcy. I should have talked to you before I walked away."

She stood, back to him, rigidity in her body. "Yes, you should have. You made a decision that wasn't just yours to make. So, where do we go from here, Doug?" She spun to face him, fighting back the tears, not wanting to show weakness. "Where do we go? We're both in the same town now."

He thrust his hands into his jeans pockets and watched her face, her eyes. "I know, Darcy. I wasn't expecting to walk into the cafe and see you there." He paused, then held out his hand. "Hi, My name's Doug Foster. Welcome to Riverville."

She looked at his hand, then up to his face, shaking her head. She reached for his hand. "Hello, Doug Foster. I'm Darcy O'Shaughnessy, and I'm not sure if what I experienced is a great welcome to your town."

Doug shook his finger at her. "Behave, Darcy. Now that we've met, I am going to be bold. Come have dinner with me at the cafe."

She tilted her head and studied him, reading the sincerity in his face and eyes. "Okay, just let me grab my sweater."

"And your purse."

"Purse?" She shook her head. "You must be talking about some other Darcy O'Shaughnessy. This girl doesn't use a purse, not any more."

He waited as she set the security system and then locked the door. He reached for her hand, but she moved away before he could catch it. Was that on purpose, he thought, or not? With Darcy, he was never sure about things.

The man watched as Doug walked away with Darcy. He had been able to avoid getting charged but he knew he would have to watch carefully when he was in this town. He would need to leave the alcohol he loved alone for the next while. That would be best. He would have a clearer head, and the voices that spoke to him would be able to be heard better. He followed the two as they walked down the street, stopping every once in a while to stare into a shop window. His mind plotting, he knew he would face them both again, and in the near future. Cops didn't do to him what that one did.

Darcy settled herself down in the booth across from Doug and pulled out the menu.

"If you're really hungry, Mac does a great special every day. Today, it's roast chicken."

Darcy looked up at him, then back at the menu. She sighed. "I don't know about this, Doug. This is hard, you know." As Mac came towards them, she stuck the menu back into the rack. "I don't know what to have. I don't have much of an appetite."

"Darcy, what'll you be having?" Mac watched her, a twinkle in his eye.

"I have no idea, Mac," she said, throwing up her hands. "Doug tells me roast chicken. What do you suggest?"

"For you, let me work a little magic and bring you something that will perk up that appetite of yours."

Mouth open in shock, she watched him walk away. A finger tapped her chin, closing her mouth. She glared at Doug, who was grinning at her.

"How did he do that?"

Doug shrugged. "That's Mac. He'll bring you something guaranteed to make you hungry. So tell me, where have you been the last few years and what have you been up to?"

She shrugged, not willing to tell him. Not yet, she thought. I don't know him well enough any more to share what I've been doing. "Working here and there and saving to set up my own store."

"How did you manage to pick this town?"

She started laughing. He stared at her, not sure if she was sane still or not. "I'm all right, Doug. It just how I managed to find this town. I laid out a map and threw a pen at it. It stuck into the name Riverville, and that's how I got here. I completely forgot it was your home town." She eyed him. "Now about you. What have you been up to?"

He laughed at her description of how she had found the town. "I like that. God directed you, did He?" He watched, concerned as she shook her head.

"No, Doug, no, He didn't. He doesn't do that for me any more."

Mac chose that moment to set their dinners in front of them. He laid a hand on Doug's shoulder. "We're praying a hedge around all of you, Doug."

"Thanks, Mac. It's appreciated. We'll certainly need it."

Darcy eyed her dinner, not quite sure what it was. "What is this?" she whispered to Doug, not wanting Mac to overhear and be offended.

He studied her plate. "I would say that's SuEllen's goulash with a little extra thrown in. It will be good, trust me."

"Trust him." She snorted and Doug laughed at her.

Partway through their meal, she laid her fork down and studied his face. "You're hurting today, Doug. Want to talk about it?"

He started to shake his head, then stopped. "It's really hard, Darcy, to fathom the evil that drove what happened today. It's far from over."

She paled. "Has he threatened more than just that town?" At his silence, her hand reached for his. "It's more than the town and the police, isn't it?"

He nodded. "I can't go into specifics, but yes, it is. He's also threatened families of emergency personnel." He dropped his fork. "Maybe this wasn't such a good idea, us having dinner."

"Doug, stop. Don't go there again. I won't let you. You chose to walk away once from me without talking to me. It will NOT happen again, get it?" He looked up, startled at the vehemence in her voice and words. "We still need to talk about what happened twelve years ago when you walked away from me just before graduation. You made the decision for us without talking to me. I won't let you do that again."

He studied her, his college sweetheart, and the lady he had never stopped loving. He finally nodded. "I did you a disservice back then, Darcy. Don't let me do it again. You've found your voice to speak up to me. Make sure you use it." He looked up as he heard steps nearing their booth.

Caleb stood watching Doug and he had to search his memory for the name. Darcy. That's what it was, Darcy. They looked like a couple he thought.

"Caleb, have you met Darcy?" Doug stood and slid onto the seat with Darcy, letting Caleb have his seat.

"No, I haven't had the pleasure yet, though Hannah has mentioned you. How's the setup going at the store?"

"Ready to open, Chief Logan. Monday will be a big day for me."

"It's Caleb, Darcy. We don't stand on formality here in Riverville, particularly if you're friends with Doug here."

Doug laughed at the expression on her face. It was good to have her back in his life. "You tracked me down for a reason, Caleb. Can you talk or do we need to go elsewhere?"

Caleb studied Darcy and made a quick decision. He had heard of her for years from Doug, without Doug realizing how much he had talked about her.

"No, we can talk, if it's okay with Darcy?" At her nod, he continued, "The first funerals are in three days. They have asked for us to provide an honour guard and also to provide ETF backup. I told them we would. It's putting a lot on your guys."

Doug nodded. "They won't care. They were ready to head down the road to there today."

Caleb nodded. "So were my guys. Frankie Brennan was heading out the door when I stopped him. This hits too close to home, Doug. And the word is out that he wants a piece of every emergency personnel in the surrounding towns, cities, and counties. No one knows who or why or where he'll strike next."

Darcy had been listening to them. Then she spoke up. "He'll strike where you least expect it, back in Greentown. This time, I would suspect a social worker or someone from the courts would be the target. You'll be looking at other towns or cities, expecting him to move on. When he moves on, he'll head for the area the farthest away and then likely move back and forth across a circle he's building around that town."

Caleb and Doug stared at her, dumbfounded at her words.

Caleb finally shook his head, watching her face and eyes. She stared back at him. "Why would you say that?"

"Because that's what he'll do. This likely stems back to an incident in his past, not necessarily from that town but from a similar town."

Caleb turned to Doug. "How's she doing that?"

Doug shook his head. How had he forgotten? "Darcy studied to be a forensics psychologist when we were in college. I suspect she's been practicing that in the past few years."

A look of pain flashed across her face. "I did and I was. I don't any more."

Caleb didn't ask what happened to take her out of her chosen field, but he knew he would be asking for her help in days and weeks to come. "Thank you, Darcy. I'll pass this on to the investigators."

She snorted. "Right and when you give them my name, they'll throw the information in the garbage."

"Darcy, what happened?" Doug's hand reached for hers.

"Don't go there, Doug. It's in the past."

Doug shared a look with Caleb who gave a subtle shake of his head.

"We'll catch up later, Darcy. Right now, Caleb, do you have time for tea and the piece of pie Mac's holding up for you?"

Caleb laughed and shook his head. "I'm heading home for a bit, then have to head back to the office."

He stood, staring at Darcy, trying to place where he knew her from, and from her words, he did know her from somewhere. He shrugged as he walked away. It would come to him at some point.

Chapter 3

Dave caught up with Doug two days later as he walked away from the department.

"What are you hearing, Doug?" Dave's eyes were concerned, although his face and demeanour didn't show it.

"Not a lot, Dave. We're still all targets but they can't pinpoint when or who will be next." He stopped in his walk. "The guys are so tense, they're snapping at one another, and they never do that."

"It's the same with us. Everybody's on edge and when a call comes in, we're almost afraid to answer it." Dave started walking again. "Where is God in this, Doug?"

Doug shrugged. "He's there, Dave. Sometimes, like Mac always says, we have to trust and wait. That's always the hard part. Trusting Someone we can't see or touch and waiting for something only He knows is about to happen. It's not easy being human."

Dave shook his head. "I have to agree."

Doug's phone sounded for a text message. He pulled it out of its holster on his belt and read it, paling as he did. He showed it to Dave, who also paled.

"She was right."

"Who was right?" Dave's puzzled voice pulled him back to the present.

"Darcy. She told Caleb this guy would hit in the same town and likely go after a social worker or someone from the courts. And he did. He hit the satellite social work office." He looked up and then turned to walk rapidly back the way they had come. "I don't know how she knew. If this gets out, she'll be in a lot of hot water and likely arrested as an accomplice."

"Don't put the cart before the horse, Doug, as your mother would say. Let's go talk with Caleb, and see what he has to say."

They searched the building, finally tracking Caleb down in his office. He waved them in and to chairs as he concluded his call.

He sat back after he hung up, deep in thought, eyes staring at his desk. Giving himself a shake, he looked at Doug. "How did she know? The police chief in Greentown just called me, asking me who gave me the information that I passed on, and if it was reliable."

Doug shrugged. "I don't know how she does it, but she's always been able to read situations and people without knowing anything or even just a little about them. It's something that just comes out of her. Can we keep her name out of it?"

Caleb nodded. "So far, we can. She's a civilian and we can use the confidential informant ticket if we have to. But I want her working with us on this. She'll be an asset we need."

"That's going to be a problem, Caleb. She's walked away from that career, and if I can remember her as well as I used to, she won't go back to it, not for anything. She looks as if it chewed her up and spit her out, and she's just starting to get herself back together."

Caleb searched through the file folders on his desk and pulled one towards him. "You're right. It's her place to tell you, if she does, but I remembered her after I got back to the office the other night. I pulled what I could. She left her position because of what happened on the job." He looked up, staring at his friend. "Don't go running over there and asking her. If I'm reading her right, it won't work."

Doug shook his head as Dave watched him, concern in his eyes and on his face. "No, she won't tell you something if she decides not to." He sighed. "If it gets out she's here, how much danger will she be in?"

"That's what isn't clear from what I have. It depends on how much the person involved wants revenge. We have enough right now to worry about."

"I'll pay her a visit and suggest she watch herself. That's not going to go over well, from what I remember." Doug looked at the door as Tom motioned for him. "I'll catch up with you two later."

They watched Doug walk away, and as Dave stood to leave, Caleb spoke.

"Watch him, Dave. I have a feeling that this is really going to get strange and wild. Doug will be a target. Don't ask me how I know, it's just a feeling I have. And Darcy's going to be involved too, much to Doug's dismay. What's going on between those two?"

Dave turned back at that. "What do you mean?"

"I tracked Doug down the other night in the cafe. They were having dinner together and looked kind of cozy."

Dave shrugged. "I would hazard a guess that's the lady Doug walked away from when he graduated from college. He said at one time he had been close to being engaged, but had left before it got to that point."

"That would make sense. Doug thinks too deep and doesn't always take into consideration the other person. They do make a cute couple."

Dave stared as Caleb uttered words he least expected to hear from him. He laughed and shook his head. "You're just a romantic at heart, Caleb. And you're right, they do make a cute couple. Catch you later." Dave walked away, still laughing, but then he sobered. If Caleb was right, then Darcy could well become a target, not just because of herself but because of Doug.

Darcy looked up from the pottery she was arranging and a pleased look crossed her face. What was Doug doing here?

"Hi."

"Darcy. Hi. Whose pottery? It's nice." Doug walked towards her.

"It's from a new client. June Abrams. She lives way out in the boonies, has been making pottery for years without selling much. She's a true artist where clay is concerned."

"That she is." He reached out a finger to run it down one of the vases. "I've never seen her work before."

"She says she has never sold it here in town. So it's a new venture for her. I think it's going to go over well with the tourists."

She looked up at his face. "But that's not why you're here."

He sighed. "No, it's not." He looked away from her, then back. "Darcy, can we talk?"

"About what?"

"About why you left the job you wanted to have so badly? That's all you talked about when we were in college."

She walked away from him to the counter. She ran her hand along the polished wood, deep in thought. His eyes watching her, he remained silent. She finally turned to him, pain evident in her eyes.

"I don't know, Doug, it just hurts so much."

"What happened, Darcy, that changed you so much?"

She stopped in front of him, eyes pleading for him not to ask. She finally shook her head.

"I guess I'm going to have to tell you at some point. Go to the back, brew us some coffee. I'll be back in a couple of minutes."

Doug hesitated, then went to do what she had asked. What is that bad, Lord? Is that what happened to her faith?

Darcy finally came through to the room she had designated as the kitchen and took the cup he held out for her and settled herself at the table.

"It's not pretty, Doug. I know you've seen a lot on your job but this is really bad." She drew in a deep breath, and in an emotionless flat voice told him of being asked to provide a profile for a local police department of someone preying on seniors. She had done that but not in time to prevent a number of deaths. When the man had been caught, he had threatened her and had been able to escape jail, running her vehicle off the road and causing injuries she wasn't ready to discuss. He had been caught and was awaiting trial.

She looked up, seeing the caring and compassion in his eyes.

"So that's what it was. I wondered if it was something like that. I don't blame you for choosing a different line of work." Doug growled as his phone dinged, indicating a text message. When he read it, he rose.

"I'm sorry, Darcy. I'm on call and we've been called out. We'll continue this conversation."

She shook her head. "No, Doug, it's over. Don't bring it up again." She watched as he hesitated beside her, then reached to draw her to her feet and into his hug. She was sure he had kissed her hair, but she must have imagined that.

Doug walked away rapidly, concerned for Darcy, and frustrated that their conversation was disrupted. He knew she meant what she said, she would never go back to it. He would have to find some way to get her to open up again.

Darcy watched as Doug left. I shouldn't have told him. Now, he'll be after me until I tell him all of it. And that's not happening. Never. She rose to put their cups in the sink and turn off the coffee pot. I am just so tired, she thought, emotions swirling through her. And it's not time yet to close up and go home.

Chapter 4

Doug sank exhausted into his office chair. The call had been canceled before they had gotten to the address, but the men on his team had been on high alert. Emotions were running high, and that always took from them. He closed his eyes for a few minutes, needing to calm himself and needing to get his head back on straight. He looked up at the knock that sounded on his door.

Caleb stood there, watching silently, then entering and shutting the door.

"Talk to me, Doug. Walk me through what happened."

"False alarm, Caleb. A false alarm. It's taking my team a long time to come down from this one. I don't know how long we can go like this."

Caleb nodded. "I know what you mean. We're feeling it across all levels." He stopped speaking for a minute, gathering his thoughts. "There was another incident today when you were out."

Doug stared at him, stern lines deepening in his face. "Where?"

"Oak City. A judge was run down crossing the street from the courthouse. He survived but will be in hospital for a long time. They have him under guard. I've talked to the police chiefs in the area. We're setting up a task force. All ETF leaders will be on it and we'll be sending in EMS and firefighter leaders as well as social workers and now court officials. It's going to be a big task trying to narrow the scope and find out who is the culprit."

Doug thought about that. "I won't walk away from my team, Caleb. They take first priority. If it comes to it, send someone else."

Caleb agreed silently as he watched his friend. "Will Darcy help out at all?"

Doug adamantly shook his head, eyes darkening as he thought of what she had told him. "Absolutely not. She told me what happened and there's no way she'll ever help again. It just about destroyed her."

Caleb stood to leave. "That's what I thought. We'll pray for a change of heart. Maybe the Lord will speak to her."

Doug stared at Caleb's back. "I don't think that will work. She's lost her faith somewhere along the way, Caleb. It's heartbreaking to see."

Darcy had watched Doug walk away and turned back to her shop. Why had she spoken so candidly to him? She had steeled her heart against him years ago and there was no way she would let him in again, not the way he had been. They were two different people now. She looked up as the door chime sounded and stepped back to the counter to watch.

The man who entered didn't really look like a tourist or someone who would be guying crafts from local artisans. She watched as he wandered the shop, finally stopping by some woodworking. He picked up a carved toy train and brought it up to pay for. Chills ran up and down her spine as she looked up into the cold eyes, dead eyes she thought.

He stared intently at her, then taking his purchase walked away. He had paid cash, so she couldn't put a name to him. She fervently hoped he never came back. She moved to the door and watched as he walked across the street, to drop into a bench facing her shop door. She shivered, feeling a presence of evil around her. If she had been a praying woman now, she would be saying them. She snorted, right, like God really cares about any of us.

Doug walked into her shop near the end of the day. She looked up, apprehension in her gaze.

"What do you want, Doug?"

He shrugged. "Nothing. Just wanted to make sure you were okay."

She stared at him, mouth open. "Why the change in heart? You didn't care twelve years ago when you walked away. Why now?"

He stared at the floor, one hand rubbing the edge of the wooden counter. He raised his eyes to hers, contrition in them. "I can never apologize or explain enough, Darcy, for how I acted. I was young and foolish and thought I was acting in your best interest. I didn't listen to the advice I was given, nor did I listen to God. What will it take for you to forgive me?"

She stared at him, mouth slightly open. The Doug she had known would never have apologized like that. She shook her head. "It doesn't happen quite like that, Doug, and you know it. I don't know if I can ever let you back in my life." She stared past him at the shadow crossing her door and shivered.

Catching her change in attention, Doug spun and strode to the door, yanking it open and exiting. He could see no one that would have caused that reaction. Slowly re-entering, he approached her.

"Care to explain, Darcy? You're jumping at shadows."

She shivered again, running her hands up and down her arms. "Not really." She turned to the back. "I'm closing up the shop for the night and heading home. Close the door behind you, Doug."

Doug shook his head. There was no way he was leaving her to close up or walk home on her own. Not with what he had just witnessed.

Darcy stopped when she saw him still standing by the counter. "What part of leave don't you understand?" She waited, toe tapping in frustration for him to move to the door.

"After what I just saw? Not happening, Darcy."

She brushed past him to hold the door open. "I don't need a keeper, Doug. I haven't had one for years and don't want one now."

Doug moved past her to stand on the sidewalk, eyes scanning the thinning crowd. He could feel eyes on him, could feel the evil, but couldn't see anyone who stood out. "You have one now, whether you want it or not. Us just having dinner together last night and talking today may have put you into the crosshairs of this maniac. I want to make sure you stay safe."

Her hand shook slightly as she locked the door and turned to him. "So leave. Run out of my life again."

"No, not happening again, Darcy. We live in the same town and we have the same friends. We can't avoid one another. Let's start over again like we did this morning. Will you have dinner with me again tonight?"

She stared at him, not believing what she had heard, then shook her head, moving past him and striding down the sidewalk. "No, Doug. Go home."

He caught up with her and with a hand to her arm, stopped her. "Darcy, you need to understand. Everyone in the EMS and police that have a close friend or relative will have those people in danger. They have been threatened."

"It's not the first time I've been threatened, Doug."

"No, it's not, but it's the first time I've had a friend threatened in that manner. At least, I would like to think of it that way." He paused, looking into the distance. "Darcy, please. Come, have at least a coffee with me at Mac's."

She shook her arm free from his and moved away, her words floating behind her.

"Find someone else, Doug. I'm sure you already have moved on."

He watched as she disappeared in the crowd, sighing as he did so. No, Darcy, there is no one else. There never will be. How do I convince you of that? Lord, she's hurting in a way I can't even imagine. Work in her heart. Soften it and bring her back to You.

Chapter 5

"How did the meeting go?" Doug turned as Caleb spoke from beside him.

He shrugged. "About as well as you could expect. Lots of paperwork, but not a whole lot of information yet. They don't really know much at all." He looked past Caleb, then back. "The chief from Greentown made an interesting comment."

"And that would be?" Caleb closed his office door.

Doug smiled. "He asked if anyone knew where Darcy O'Shaughnessy was now. He wanted her to work on the case for him."

"Really?" Caleb wasn't surprised. He had been asked the same question. "And I don't suppose you let on you knew exactly where she was."

"No, I didn't. She's a civilian now, though she likely always was. It won't go over well if he knows she's here in town and isn't willing to help."

Caleb shook his head as his phone rang. Looking at the number, he answered, his face paling as he listened. Doug sat up straighter. This was not going to be good news, he thought.

"What town? And who?"

Caleb looked stunned but thoughtful as he laid his phone back on the desk. "Birch Creek. This time is was paramedics. Thankfully, no deaths or major injuries this time. They can't figure out how that was avoided."

"God."

Caleb smiled. "I'm sure you're right. Now back to what we were talking about. Darcy won't help, I already have gathered that, not unless we force her to. I'm not at that point yet, though that may come."

"This guy is moving around. Darcy said he would. I hate to think of him hitting here."

Caleb nodded. "We have too many friends and relatives in the emergency services."

Doug stopped outside Darcy's shop later that afternoon. He desperately needed a break and hope he would find it here. The bell tinkled over his head as he entered. Darcy looked around from where she was talking with a customer and, brows raised, gave him a questioning look. He wandered through her shop, stopping every once in a while to really study a piece of art that caught his attention. She had obtained some beautiful pieces, he thought.

"Can I help you find something, sir?" A gurgle of amusement rippled through her voice.

"You have some really great pieces here, Darcy. This should do well with the tourists."

She nodded. "It already is. And the online store is taking off. I'm not sure I'll have enough merchandise to complete all the orders I'm taking in." She looked around, contentment on her face. "I never felt like this with my last position. I always felt judged and on edge."

Doug nodded. "We get the same with our job. You can't please everyone, even though you want to." He looked down at her. "What time does your shop close?"

"In about ten minutes." She looked up at him and shook her head. "No, Doug, not dinner. Not again."

He smiled, and a finger came up to touch her face. "Yes. I'll even say please and thank you if that works."

She shook her head. "Not at your uncle's, if I were to agree. People would think we were dating or something."

He shook his head. "No, they're not like that here. They would just think we're old friends renewing a friendship. That's what I've been telling those who have seen us and asked."

"Then it's no wonder I'm getting the looks and smiles that I am." She sighed. "If you insist, I guess I will. Just let me lock away the cash receipts from today and make sure everything is set for the night."

"What can I do?" Doug wanted to help her.

She shook her head. "Just stand by the door. I'll be right back."

Doug held the door for her as they left the restaurant.

"Thank you, Doug. That was nice." She stopped to look at him, then looked down the street. She hadn't brought her car today, expecting to be home before dark. She never liked being out after dark, especially if she was on foot.

"I enjoyed that. Where's your car?"

"I didn't drive today. I expected to be home before dark."

He picked up on the hint of fear and apprehension in her voice, something he never had heard before. "Come on, then. Walk with me. I'll give you a lift home."

She shook her head. "No, I'll be okay."

Doug stopped her with a hand on her arm. "No, I'm giving you a lift home."

She finally shrugged, staring around. What was it she could feel? She didn't like the fear and evil she could sense around her.

"Whereabouts is your home?"

She looked over at him. "You mean, you don't know?" When he shook his head, she laughed. "I happen to live down the street from a police lieutenant's mother. She talks about him all the time."

"You bought the White's house?" At her nod, he continued, "Mom never said who had bought it."

He waited at the busiest street corner in town for the light to change. As it changed to green, he entered the intersection, never seeing the large truck that had suddenly picked up speed as the driver spied his vehicle and recognized it. Too late, he heard the roar of an engine, saw the lights and felt the impact as the truck rammed the back of his truck, spun it around and kept going. He faintly heard Darcy's scream, then blackness closed in.

Caleb stood near the ambulance as he watched the paramedics working on Doug. He was still unconscious, and that worried him. He needed him on the job right now and that didn't look like it was going to be possible. He turned to scan the area, searching for the culprit. The truck had been found abandoned two blocks away, and of course, he thought, stolen earlier that day.

Dave approached him. "We're ready to transport, Caleb. You've got an officer ready to go with us?" At Caleb's nod, he turned to the other ambulance just pulling away. "Darcy's really shaken, and I don't think it's just from this accident."

Caleb shook his head. "I can tell you this, it's not. From what I understand, she had a really serious accident a couple of years ago. It nearly killed her."

Dave whistled. "No wonder she's like she is. Catch up with us when you can."

Darcy pulled the heated sheet up tighter to her chin. She couldn't stop the shakes, couldn't stop feeling chilled. The memories had resurfaced, and she was afraid she would fall apart and end up admitted and on medication again. She looked over at the door, cracked open just a bit. She silently shifted off the stretcher and moved quietly to the door, pulling it open just a bit more. The doctor had been in and had said he wanted her to stay for a while. That wasn't happening, she decided. Dave had been in and said Doug was being examined but he didn't have any more information than that.

Peeking out the door, Darcy breathed a sigh of relief. No one was around. That meant she could run from there and find her sanctuary at home. As she disappeared around the corner of a hallway, Caleb caught a glimpse of her and stopped short. Had he really seen her? Then he nodded. Of course he had. All the ladies in this town ran when they were scared or didn't want to answer questions. He should know that by now.

The Emergency Room physician was headed for her room and stopped short when he saw Caleb. "Not there?"

Caleb shook his head. "No. Just let me know what you want me to tell her, give me whatever medications you want her to take, and I'll get them to her."

"She really shouldn't be out there on her own. She was too shaken to be safe walking."

"Did she tell you she had had another serious accident in the last couple of years? Didn't think she did. Tonight would have brought back far too many memories."

Caleb turned and sought out Doug's room. He eyed the officers in the waiting room and milling around the hallway. At least, he should be safe here, Caleb thought.

Doug groaned as he moved his head, consciousness returning to him. He hurt and he didn't know why. Cracking open his eyes, he squinted, not quite sure where he was. Movement to his left caused him to start, sending the pain to a new level.

Caleb watched as Doug grimaced, hating that he was hurting. Heal him, Lord, heal not just his body. His heart needs healing too.

"Doug. Wake up, buddy."

"Caleb. Where am I? I hurt, too."

"You're in the hospital, Doug. Do you remember what happened?"

Doug went to shake his head and groaned again. "No, I don't remember past being in the office this afternoon. What time is it?"

"It's after midnight. You've been out for about six or seven hours."

"What did happen?"

"Someone deliberately rammed your truck tonight at the main intersection. You don't remember anything?"

"No. Was I alone?"

Caleb hesitated before he spoke, knowing that Doug would want to get up and leave to find Darcy. "No, Darcy was with you."

"Darcy! I don't remember that. How is she?"

Caleb smiled, even though Doug couldn't see it. "She checked herself out and has left already. Is there something I should know?"

Doug squinted against the lights again and sighed. "Yeah, I guess there is. I just hope she forgives me. She was almost killed a couple of years ago by an assailant when he ran her off the road. I think she still has anxiety issues related to that."

"I suspect you're right." Caleb pulled his phone out to look at a text message just coming in. His face whitened and anger grew within him.

"What town did he hit now, Caleb?"

Caleb looked down at Doug. Somehow Doug had figured it out. "Willow Bay. No casualties, though it wasn't for him not trying. He set a bomb off near the fire department, not realizing they were out at a fire."

"Where is he going to hit next? And it doesn't make sense that he's choosing so many different ways of hitting at us."

"I think that's all part of his game. I would like to hear Darcy's take on that."

Doug's eyes slid shut. "That won't be happening. Check on her, Caleb. Make sure she's all right. She bought White's house just down from Mom's. Where is Mom, by the way?"

"She's in the waiting room, being entertained. She'll be back in a few minutes."

Caleb stood on Darcy's porch and rang the doorbell again. "Darcy, it's Caleb Logan. If you're there, open the door, please."

He saw movement, then the door cracked open just a bit. "Caleb, what are you doing here?"

"Can I come in for a minute, Darcy? I have some medication and instructions for you from the hospital."

She opened the door enough for him to enter, then closed it again, heading back for the living room. A low light was burning, just enough for him to assess her. Doug was right. She was hurting.

He handed her the bag he had been given. "They want you to take the pain medications on a certain schedule and they included something for nausea."

She tossed the bag on the table. "Not happening, Caleb. I've had enough of that kind of medications to last a lifetime. Now, why are you really here?"

Doug was right, she's not making it easier, Caleb thought. "Doug asked me to check on you, to make sure you were okay."

"Like he really cares!" Sarcasm bit through her words. "No, that's not why you're here. Your culprit or whatever you want to call him struck again and you want me to help. No, Caleb. I don't do that any more. I left it behind years ago. Now, you can see yourself out.   The door will lock behind you."

He stood on her porch and looked around. Something didn't seem right, but he couldn't put it finger on it. He shook his head at the way she had dismissed him. Doug, he thought, you're in for quite the ride to get your lady back in your life.

Chapter 6

Doug sank gratefully onto the couch in Caleb's office. Against medical advice, he was there. Tom watched as he moved slowly, knowing that Doug just wasn't well.

"Doug, you need to be at home, not here."

Doug shook his head and regretted that. The concussion was mild but the headache was strong. Maybe he hadn't made the best choice, coming here, the way his body ached. He needed to be here, though.

"Where do we stand now, Caleb?"

"About where we were. This guy is good. He's doing what Darcy said he would, moving across from one side of a circle to another and hitting towns on the way."

"That scares me, Caleb. If she's right, we'll be one of the next ones."

Caleb nodded. "I know. I've been meeting with our emergency services, trying to prepare our best we can. But he's shown that he will adapt and change, depending on the target he's after. And that's not something we can predict."

Tom spoke up. "Not really, but if we take a look at what each part of the emergency service does, then maybe we can narrow down how we might be hit."

"What do you mean, Tom?" Caleb waited for him to continue.

"For example, the police. He went after them with weapons. The social work office—fire. The judge who I hear deals with a lot of drunk drivers, he was run down. The fire department - a bomb with ensuing fire. I can see him going after the paramedics with an accident or something life threatening. Have you added in the search and rescue teams?"

Caleb shook his head. "Now, that's one team I would never have thought of. There is just such an expanse to look at. Where do we start?"

"That's the problem. We don't know. The task force is pulling every name that has ever made a threat against one of the services and that numbers into the hundreds, if not thousands. There are just too many names."

Caleb agreed, then rose to open his office door at a commotion outside of it. He was back in a minute.

"So where do we start then, once again, to narrow down the field of players?"

"Oak City is starting to run names through the databases, but they're not hopeful they'll come up with much." Tom shook his head. "I just fear, Caleb, that we won't find him in time, that he'll take more lives." Tom rose and left on those words.

Doug looked at Caleb through blurry eyes. "He's right. We're not going to be in time."

Caleb shook his head. "I agree. Now come on, let's get you to your Mom's. You can't stay on your own."

"Wait, Caleb. Did you see Darcy last night, and is she okay?"

"I saw your lady, and yes, she's okay. She kicked me out of her house and as much as told me to leave her alone. Hannah laughed like everything when I told her and said she really wanted to make this lady her friend.   And Hannah also said God was watching out for you two last night."

"He was."

Darcy stood in her shop, jumping at every little noise. She couldn't continue like this, she thought.   She had felt safe and secure here. Now she didn't. Had that been him last night?   Or a family member or friend?   She couldn't go to the police and ask. She just didn't have it in her any more to keep answering the same questions and seeing the same doubt in the eyes of the law.

She turned as she heard the doorbell tinkle and frowning, walked towards the man who had entered.   He was not a customer, she could tell.

"Can I help you?"

"Darcy O'Shaughnessy?" At her nod, he continued, "Doug described you well. I'm Detective Frankie Brennan.   Caleb asked me to talk to you about your accident last night. Somehow, he got the impression you wouldn't talk to him." Frankie grinned at her.

She shook her head and threw up her hands. "Now, why would he think that? I can't remember much, it happened so quickly." She jumped as he moved to take his notebook out of his jacket.

"I'm sorry. I didn't mean to startle you."

"That's okay. I'm jumping at every little sound today. Something just seems off here in the store and I can't put my finger on it."

Frankie stilled, then watched her intently. "Describe to me what you're thinking and feeling."

She sighed, knowing that the detective mode had just kicked in. "It's just that things seem to have been shifted slightly from where I had them set." She walked through the building with him, indicating where she had noticed something off. He left her to check the doors and windows.

"Do you have a basement, Darcy?" She shook her head. "An attic? No? Then where's your storage at?"

She led him to the back room she had set aside for storage. He looked around the neat area, then moved towards a door at the back. "Was this locked last night?"

She nodded. "It was and it has an alarm on it."

"Not any more, it doesn't. Someone tampered with it." He turned to see her face pale even more than it had been.

"Someone broke in? You mean, they could have been in here when I came in today?"

Frankie was at her side, hand under her arm to hold her upright. He steered her back to the kitchen and into a chair. "He not likely would have hung around. You don't have anything in your shop that can be taken and sold readily. I'll have one of our crime lab techs take a look around and see if there are any prints there, other than yours. I know the fellow who set up your security. He'll come back and make it even more secure. I would suggest adding cameras."

She nodded, suddenly afraid. "Frankie, can we not do the crime scene tech bit? I don't think he'll be back."

He shrugged, puzzled that she refused. "We can, but it won't help us catch this guy."

She nodded. "I know. I just don't want that done."

She finally wandered around her home again later that day. Had she made a mistake moving here, she wondered? She hoped not, suddenly feeling the urge to pray. She shrugged it off. It hadn't worked for her in the past. There was no reason to think it would now.

She turned as the doorbell rang. She wasn't expecting anyone. Peeking out, she stepped back in surprise, before unlocking and opening the door.

"And just what are you doing here?" She looked around him to see who had brought him to her house.

Doug grinned, then grimaced. "Mom sent me down to ask you to come to dinner. She heard you were with me last night and feels she needs to take care of you too. See? She's standing on the walk, waiting for us to head back there."

Darcy shook her head. "You just don't give up, do you? Now, you've recruited your mother."

Doug winced at her words, then spoke a bit more sharply than he meant to. "Darcy, it's not all about who's out to try your patience or make you do something you don't want to. It's about others giving to you because they want to. Mom has asked, knowing that you won't feel like cooking. If you don't want to come, just say so and I'll leave."

She stepped back in surprise. The Doug she had known would never have spoken to her like that. "I'm sorry, Doug. You're right. It was kind of your mother to ask. Let me get my keys. You look like you need to be sitting down, not chasing me down."

A ghost of a grin spread across his face. "Now, lady, that I would enjoy once again, chasing you down."

She shook her head at him, then tucking her hand into his elbow, walked with him back down the street.

The man stood and watched as they passed by him. They didn't see him, standing well back from the road and in the shadows. So, he thought, they are a couple. Now that makes it more interesting and challenging. What can I come up with? They will both pay. Last night didn't teach them anything. He moved away from them and headed for his vehicle, off to the next town he had plotted revenge in. Riverville was to be the last one and the biggest and best one.

Chapter 7

Doug eased his body down into his chair in his office. It had been a week since the accident and he was still sore and confined to desk work. That didn't sit well, not when the threat was still out there. Whoever it had been was quiet at the moment, but Doug expected a call to come in at any time listing new casualties.

He looked up as Tom tapped at his door and then entered.

"Tom, what's the word?"

"Nothing new, Doug. That worries me."

"Me, too. How are the men?"

Tom shrugged. "They're hurting for the ones lost and for their families." Tom studied Doug. "And how are you feeling?"

Doug shrugged. "Sore and, before you say it, I know I shouldn't be here, but I have to be."

Tom nodded. "I know you do." They both looked as Caleb appeared in the doorway, then entered and closed the door.

"Caleb, that doesn't look good." Doug studied Caleb's face.

Caleb shook his head. "It's not. He's back, this time in the county outside Oak City. He attacked the county officers when they were investigated an accident. Three are in hospital."

Doug sat back in his chair. "No deaths?"

"Thankfully, not time, but it's only a matter of time before it happens again." Caleb hesitated before he continued. "I'm sending you over to help with the investigation, Doug. You're not going to be able to work your normal tasks for a while yet. The task force has finally settled on working from Oak City. We're setting up down in the old pharmacy."

Doug nodded. "Yes, okay. It's not what I want but I guess it will do. I just hate not being with my guys."

"I know. Once you have medical clearance come back and talk with me.

Tom, that leaves you a man short on your team. Doug and you talk about it and then let me know what you want to do.”

They watched Caleb walk away, heaviness in his steps, then turned to discuss how they would handle the next few days.

Darcy walked away from her shop, glad the day was over. It had been a busy one, but speculation had been rampant over what was happening to the emergency forces in the nearby towns. It had tired her out, listening and having to keep the anxiety she felt in check.

She turned as she heard her name. Doug was walking towards her. She studied his face, noting that the bruising was fading.

“Darcy, how are you? I kept trying to get in to see you today.”

She shrugged. “About the same as when you asked this morning when you saw me at Mac’s. How are you after being at work all day?”

He smiled but didn’t reply, just watched the sun playing across her face and hair. He had been a fool, he thought, to walk away from her.

"About like that, is it? Doug, why don't you go home? I don't need an escort."

Doug sighed, knowing it would be an uphill battle to get back into her life. "I just wanted to talk with you. Have dinner with me?"

She shook her head. "You just don't give up, do you?"

Puzzled, he stared at her. She grumbled to herself, then nodded. "Just dinner, then I'm heading home. I have a lot of paperwork to do that I didn't get to today."

Their steps turned towards the cafe, neither one seeing the man standing in the shadowy doorway behind them. He watched as they entered the cafe, laughter floating back to him. One day, he vowed, they would pay.

Darcy looks up as Mac approached them.

"What will you be having this fine night, Darcy? You're one I can't predict what you'll be having, you know, and that's the way it is."

She laughed up at him and his nonsense. "Today, Mac, make it just a salad and a tea, please."

Doug shook his head at her. "You need more than that."

She frowned at him, hazel eyes sparking. "Don't go there, Doug. I know what I need and don't need to eat."

He sat back, hands up in self defence. "Sorry, Darcy, don't bite."

She shook her head. "I didn't bite, and you know that. Anyway, it's your own fault. Now behave."

Talk wandered through a variety of subjects before Doug noticed that she seemed on edge and uneasy. He rose and taking her hand, pulled her through the cafe kitchen and out that back door.

"Doug," she protested. "We didn't pay for our meals."

He shrugged. "Then pay the next time you're in. Mac won't let you, I guarantee you that."

"It's not right, Doug."

Doug shrugged, already knowing that his uncle had paid for their meals himself. "I'll pay him the next time I see him."

"I'll never be able to go in there and eat again. You made me feel like a thief." She broke away from him and walked rapidly through the parking lot.

Doug ran after her and pulled her to a stop. "Darcy, you need to understand something. Mac couldn't care less if you paid for your meal or not. You were with me. He never charges whoever is eating with one of his family members, if he can get away with that. It's who he is."

Darcy stiffened under his hand, but he refused to remove it from her arm. "It just doesn't seem right, Doug. How does he stay in business?"

Doug shrugged. "He does all right. That's just the way he has always been." Doug looked around, his dark eyes scanning the area at a feeling of being watched. "Listen, let me take you home, if you're walking. We still haven't caught this guy and I'm worried about you."

She snorted at that. "Don't be, Doug. I'm a big girl and can take care of myself."

"Darcy, would you stop with the attitude? That's not the lady I remember."

"No, I'm not that lady any more, Doug, and I'm getting the impression you don't like who I've become." She pulled away from him and walked rapidly down the street.

Doug sighed as he watched her, then ran once again to catch up with her. "Darcy, wait. You're taking offence where none is offered."

She refused to look at him, as she came to a halt. He watched as her face tightened and she began to scan the area.

"Darcy?"

She turned, fright in her eyes. "Doug, who is out there? Someone has been watching me for the last couple of weeks, since I had that run-in with that man outside the shop. I can feel him. There's an evil around this area." Her eyes turned from him and her faced whitened. "What have I done? Why did I ever come here?"

Doug scanned the area quickly, then pulled her towards his truck, shoving her into the passenger side and quickly rounding the vehicle to climb in himself.

"You did nothing wrong, Darcy. I can feel it too, and I don't think it's directed at you." He watched as she struggled to regain her composure, to tamp down the anxiety he could see rising within her. He reached for her hand, and she jumped when he touched it.

She turned her eyes to him. "Doug, I didn't tell you everything when we were talking about my accident. I have been left with anxiety that can lead to panic attacks. I refuse to take medication for it. I was threatened by a former employer that if I didn't, he would make sure everyone who asked for my help and checked with him would know about that and that he would ruin me. I always felt that he didn't like the fact I had led investigators in the right direction on my last task, where he hadn't been able to."

Doug cringed inwardly at her words, anger beginning to build inside him at the cruelty of the man. "He told you this when you were recovering from the accident, which by the way would be considered an assault?"

She nodded, apprehension growing in her eyes. She turned to reach for the door handle, ready to leave.

Doug's hand settled on her shoulder. "In no way, shape or form are you damaged goods. Caleb wants you to come work for him. The police chief in Greentown has been trying to track you down; he's desperate for your input. And me?" Here he paused, waiting for her to turn back to him, eyes caressing the profile she had to him. "I'm thinking I'm a fortunate man to have you back in my life, even just as a friend. I've always regretted the way I handled it, and was too stubborn and full of pride to humble myself to ask for your forgiveness. I wasted so much of our time together, Darcy."

Darcy continued to stare out the window, digesting what Doug had said to her. "Did Caleb really say that?"

"He did. He knows you're not likely to, given the shop you've got going and that is taking off so quickly and so well. That is a blessing in this town. You've helped so many people."

"And the police chief in Greentown? He's really looking for me in a good way?"

"He is, Darcy. What did this guy do to you anyway?"

She shook her head. "Not going there, Doug. So what was it Caleb wanted me to do for him?"

"I think he wanted to pick your brain and see what other information you could provide for him, suggestions as to what we should be looking for. We've got so much information we're wading through, it's taking forever."

"How many more towns has he hit?"

"As of now, I think we're at six or seven. He's hit a different branch of law enforcement or a connection to law enforcement in each area. Twice, he's gone after paramedics."

She turned to him, eyes not focusing on him. He could see that she was lost on a tangent. "Can you bring Caleb to my place on a pretext of some kind? I don't want to take time away from Hannah and his boys though."

Doug nodded. "We can figure something out." He pulled out his cell to make the call when her next words stopped him. "What did you say?"

"I said to tell Caleb to have the police chief from Greentown contact me through him. Maybe it would be a good idea if they were together. I don't want it in an official meeting though or in an official place."

Doug nodded. "Are you sure, Darcy? I don't want to pressure you."

"You're not. I don't want to be in that line of work any more, I can't do it. But these are extraneous circumstances, and I would be remiss if I refused to help." She looked away as he made the call to Caleb.

"He'll call when he gets something set up. He asked where you wanted to meet."

"Somewhere we won't be recognized or where people would comment on our meeting."

Doug looked at his phone as the ring interrupted them. "Caleb. What did you come up with?" His eyes sought her as he listened. "All right, we'll both be there. If anything changes, I'll let you know."

She watched as he clicked the phone off thoughtfully and stuffed in back into its holster.

"Where?"

"There a little cafe about an hour from here. Caleb and the chief meet there on a regular basis. It has a back room we can use." He reached for her hand, feeling the familiar contours of it and the new roughness and scars on it. "Are you sure, Darcy?"

She hesitated, then nodded. "I think so. This time and this time only." She didn't tell him it was because he was on the front lines and a target. There was no way she was opening herself up to that again.

Doug drove through town in a circuitous manner, prompting the comment from Darcy that he really didn't seem to know where he was going. He just laughed at her, keeping his eyes on the mirrors and traffic around him.

"How's the store doing?" He watched her out of the corner of his eye.

"It's really doing well. I'm likely going to have to hire a clerk soon, so I can keep on top of suppliers and products. Word is getting out and I'm getting more calls every day from artists from all around the area. Most of them, I would put into the online store."

"I'm glad it's working out." He took a chance and added, "And I'm glad you're here in Riverville."

She stared at him, then turned to the window, no comment coming from her. Doug wondered at that, she usually had a comeback for everything.

"Here we are, Darcy." Doug pulled around to the back of the cafe and parked. "Caleb's here. He said for us to go in through the kitchen, he would have cleared the way for us."

Caleb stood from the table he had been sitting at and watched intently as Doug and Darcy entered the room. He could feel the concern and apprehension coming from her, and knowing how she had last been treated, he certainly understood

"Darcy, thank you for meeting with us." Caleb gestured to their chairs. "Bill Watson will be here shortly. I understand you've met?"

"We have, when I first started working. Unfortunately by the time I got involved, it was already too late for the little girl, but they were able to catch her kidnapper." She stopped speaking and got tense as she heard the door open behind her and Doug and Caleb greeting the man who entered.

Bill Watson stopped at the other side of the table and studied the young woman he had met many years ago. She's been beaten up pretty badly, he thought, beaten up, chewed up, spit out and run over. And it's a real shame. She's so good at what she did.

"Darcy. It's good to see you again."

"Bill.   I just wish it was under different circumstances."

"I wondered where you were now. I understand you have a really nice shop going. I'll bring my wife and daughters over one day. They love the type of merchandise you are handling."

"There's an online store as well, Bill. You don't have to make the trip."

"Ah, but you see, I want to. I'll only say this once, and these two fine gentlemen will be my witness. You got a very raw deal. Everyone around you felt the same way. That treatment has trickled through to the departments around, and I can guarantee you that every one of us would fight for you."

She blinked, surprised at his words, then shook her head. "It's in the past. Now, what do you want from me tonight?"

The three men exchanged glances, not surprised at her words, as they settled themselves down at the table and prepared to sort through what she presented.

Caleb handed her a folder. "This contains the latest information that our task force investigators have confirmed. They've been working around the clock, trying to find this man before he hits somewhere else."

She nodded, then opened the folder and began to read, the men's voices dying away from her hearing. She always gave total intent concentration of what she was reading and studying. Doug watched the conflicting emotions playing across her face.

She stopped, finger on a paragraph. "Bill, what were they trying to find out when they went back to the scene of the ETF takedown?"

Bill was surprised that she had picked that up. He had almost missed it himself. "They were looking to see if he was from the area or had friends there. It was neither. It looks as if he just chose it in random."

She shook her head. "No, it's not random. It can't be." She looked around, frustrated.

"What do you need, Darcy?" Doug spoke up, knowing that she was looking for something.

"I need a pen and something to write on. I hate this, not being prepared."

Caleb slid pens and pads of paper towards her. "We were." He smiled as she looked up at him.

"Thank you." She read through the report, then went back to the beginning. "This is my copy? I can mark it up all I want?" At the affirmative answer, she began to read through the material, making notes and marking the document. Finally, she sat back exhaustion on her face.

They waited while she gathered her thoughts. Doug rose, left and came back with a cup of tea for her. He knew her preference when she was stressed like she was.

She looked up at them, then back at her notes.

"Are you really ready to hear what I have to say? Because if you're not, I'm out of here."

Caleb and Bill exchanged a glance, then Bill spoke. "We are, Darcy."

"Ok, then let me go through it and then ask questions. First, about him. He is not a loner, but has few friends. Likely raised in foster care or by someone with little funds to raise him, causing resentment on their part. He had little as a child. I would suspect that he had been removed from a bad home situation, single parent or parents separated."   She stopped, eyes dropping to her notes as whiteness gripped her face.

"Darcy, what is it?"

She shook off whatever it was that had come over her. "You may be looking for someone who had a parent murdered, perhaps by a spouse or significant other. He will be in a low-paying job, not likely through high school, definitely not college. As to drugs or alcohol, I would suggest the latter."

She stopped again to gather her thoughts. "I am getting so many conflicting images and sensations that I can't be sure which is what I should be giving you.   I think it's stemming from him, that he has such conflict inside him that it comes through no matter where he is or where he's around.

"As to where the first incident occurred, you have suggested, Bill, that he had no connection there?"

Bill nodded, wondering where she was heading.

"My feeling is that you need to go back there, to look about 15 years or so, and find out if you can who lived there and had contact with the police on a regular basis. This is where you're going to find him, by going back to police records a number of years ago. I know you think he's not from Greentown, but my feeling is that is what he wants you to think.

"As to why he's going after the police? Quite frankly, he blames them for losing his parents, for not having what he wants in life. That hatred has festered and spread like a bad infection to encompass all emergency personnel, social workers, court officials. He will keep adding to that list, just because he can, because someone offends him. It won't stop until you stop him."

Caleb took in what she was saying, making notes as she talked. "What about a probable location for him?"

Darcy shook her head as she looked at him. "You won't like it, Caleb. You all think he's moving around, or staying central. I suspect he's moving out towards the edge of where's he causing the destruction." She stopped, sadness covering her face. "Where do I think he is? Riverville."

Caleb's pen dropped to the table as he stared at her. "Riverville?"

She nodded. "And I think we have had contact with him at some point. There are times I have felt watched, felt an evilness I have never ever felt in town. That's him."

Bill exchanged a glance with Caleb, then nodded. He knew how accurate her readings were.

"Can you give us anything else, Darcy?"

"At the moment, no. But I'm sure I'll come up with something." She reached into her pocket and handed Bill a business card. "I'm not coming back officially, Bill, but this affects the town I'm living in. I can't do this anymore."

Bill studied her card, then looked up at her. "I think you could, but you are looking at a different direction in your life. Just let me ask a favour. Please work with us on this."

She nodded, then sighed. "I know you can't keep my name out of it. But how do I keep my new life quiet and private? The news media ate me for breakfast, lunch and supper and I don't want that happening ever again. I don't want to have to pull up stakes and move again."

Bill watched her, then turned his head as he caught a look on Doug's face. His eyes narrowed and he saw Caleb watching Doug's face as well. He nodded. No, Darcy, you won't be pulling up stakes and moving on.

Caleb watched the two seated near the end of the table. Please, Lord, heal their hearts and bring them both back to You in a deeper way. Renew Darcy's love for You again. Keep us safe.

"I can put this out in a way that no one will know you talked to us. There may be questions and some may guess it was you, but without confirmation, you won't be on the front line." Caleb was adamant that she would not bear any blame or fault or concern over this.

"Thank you." Darcy stood. "If that's all, I think Doug needs to take me back to my home. It's been too long a day."

Doug nodded to the two police chiefs, then led Darcy out the back way from the room and back to his truck. Tucking her inside, he hesitated for a moment, watching her through the window. He climbed behind the wheel and pulled out of the parking lot, heading for home.

"Why, Darcy?"

She turned to him. "Why what, Doug?"

"Why'd you decide to help?"

She shrugged. "I just had to. Doug, I have felt someone watching me since I had that run-in with that man a few weeks ago. Could it be him?"

"You're just telling me now? I don't know, Darcy. It could be or it could be someone else. Next time, call me."

She shook her head. "I don't think so, Doug. You need to stop hovering over me."

He grinned. "Is that what I'm doing?"

She snorted, causing him to laugh. "You know right well you are. You've done it enough I'm starting to get questions, like, Where's that Doug? He needs to be with you. Or, you and Doug really need to come for dinner tonight. You know how your town talks."

By this time, Doug was laughing. "Well, whoever asked us to dinner, we could go and stop that question."

"Don't even suggest that. I can barely tolerate that woman."

Doug laughed even harder. "I know who you mean. She's like that with everyone. She means well."

Darcy glared at him again. "Not happening."

Chapter 8

Caleb and Bill digested what Darcy had told them, then looked at one another.

"Are we really going to be able to keep her name out of it?" Caleb was skeptical that they could.

"I'm going to do my best, Caleb. She got a raw deal the last time she did this. And I don't want that to happen again."

"Is he still on the force?"

Bill shook his head. "No, he took early retirement after that fiasco. He waited too long to ask for help and then blamed her for the lives that were lost. It was either retirement or a demotion. He took retirement. He blamed her for that too."

"Was it really that suspect that ran her off the road? I read a report that suggested he denied it, that he was nowhere near her."

Bill sat back. "Now, that's interesting, Caleb. I'm hearing scuttlebutt that it wasn't him, but the sergeant and that he paid the suspect to take the blame. Let me look into that. If we can clear that up, maybe it will free her up to work with us again."

Caleb nodded, then stacked his paperwork back into his briefcase. Checking his watch, he sighed. He wouldn't be home in time to spend any with his boys, and he and they all needed that. He would free up some time in the next few days.

Doug tapped at Caleb's office door two days later, face set into stern lines. Caleb motioned him in.

"Where'd he hit?"

"In the hills outside Freetown, where a police search and rescue unit was doing training. I don't have an exact total yet, but we have a couple officers dead and more down."

Caleb sank back. "Are we any closer to this guy?"

Doug shook his head, then handed Caleb a piece of paper. "This was on my desk this morning."

Caleb took it, apprehension in his movements. As he read, his heart chilled.

"How did he know we met?"

Doug shrugged. "I have no idea. None of us talked. I was careful not to be followed and I went over every inch of the truck checking for any tracking devices."

"Bill and I went in and out the back way, just like you. We didn't see anyone, and Ray had turned off the cameras while we were there."

"Somehow, he's finding us and following us. Darcy mentioned that she feels like she is being watched all the time. She thinks it was that passerby she had a problem with. I pulled his file. He's not from here and no one seems to have seen him since."

Caleb thought about that. "We can't do much if there's no one we can pinpoint that's doing that." He looked up as Frankie appeared in his doorway. "Frankie, what's up?"

Frankie looked grimmer than they had ever saw him. "We just got hit. The search and rescue group that got ambushed? We had an officer training with them."

Caleb hesitated. "A victim or a casualty?"

"She's in hospital in the trauma unit. They won't say if she'll make it or not."

"Keep me updated and let me know where to find her family."

"Will do."

Doug followed Frankie, headed for his own team. He knew they would have heard. Lord, keep us safe. Give me the words I need to bring comfort, strength and courage.

Darcy looked up as Doug stopped beside her and then sank down on the park bench. He had tracked her down to the city park where she had gone to enjoy some sunshine.

"That bad, Doug?" When he nodded, she set aside her sandwich and reached for his hand, just sitting with him in silence.

"He got one of ours while she was training today. She may not make it." He couldn't continue.

She let him sit in silence, then said, "So what happens now, Doug? Are they able to find out any more on him?"

He shook his head. "They're really working with what you gave Bill the other night, but it's taking time to work through it all. He's not sure how far they'll get before he strikes again."

"So, you tell me, why does God allow this?" She stood and stared down at him, her lunch forgotten on the bench. "How does a loving God allow death and destruction?"

She turned then and walked back to her shop, fear coursing through her. He was coming for her, she could tell. Which one would find her first, the sergeant or the man who kept hitting at emergency services?

Doug watched her walk away, ready to go after her, but knowing she didn't want him to. She needed time to come to terms with what she had asked, and he had to give it to her. He reached for his phone and then headed to the department on a run. An ETF call. Please, Lord, keep us safe.

Doug went through the room his men had gathered in, talking to each one. When he was finished, he stood and stared around. They were taking a beating, the apprehension growing with each call. Lord, how much can we take? And how do the men without faith get through this? He turned as Tom came towards him and then nodded for the door.

"What's the word from the men, Tom?"

"They're scared, Doug, not scared enough to quit, though with some of the younger ones it's getting close. The older ones, they're in for the long haul. They won't leave voluntarily."

"And it doesn't matter what service it is. How is he finding out where the teams are training or where certain people are going to be?"

"That a good question. He's likely picking a target and then tracking them until he feels the time is right to hit. With the teams, he's setting up some of the ambushes. With the other, it may be a chance taken on something overheard."

Doug nodded. "I think you're right." He sighed. "Track me down if you need me. My desk is piled down with paperwork."

Tom smiled. "Better you than me."

Doug piled the last of the paperwork together for his secretary, then turned to the calls he needed to make. His hand stilled. Now that really was a voice from the past, that name. How had Betty James tracked him down? He hadn't thought of her since he had graduated from college and finished her classes on suspect identification.

He dialed her number. He could hear the age in her voice now when she answered. He was trying to figure out how old she would be now and knew she was definitely a senior.

"Mrs. James, it's Doug Foster. You called earlier today and asked me to call you back."

"Doug Foster! How are you? You were one of the best students I ever had in all my years of teaching, if not the best."

He grinned in pleasure at her compliment. "You made learning so easy and so fun." They chatted for a few minutes, then Doug asked, "You called me. What's up?"

Her voice still, and he could hear the hesitation over the phone. "I had called to speak with someone, and they put me through to you. I wasn't sure if it was the same Doug Foster I taught, but I am glad it is. I have heard about what's happening, not much more than what's in the media, but I have a name I wondered if you could check out. He was always a little strange, aloof, and had the attitude that the world owed him. He was a couple of years behind you, so I don't think you knew him." She passed on the name, as much as she could remember about him. "Now, Doug, what about you? Married? Family?"

Doug smiled, though he could feel the disappointment in himself because of his choices. "No, not yet."

"And what about that lovely girl you were so crazy about? Darcy, wasn't it?"

Doug sighed. "It was Darcy. We parted ways just as we graduated. But she's living here in my town now."

"Don't let her get away from you this time. If either of you are out my way, stop in."

Doug hung up the phone and stared at the paper he had been writing on. Could it

be that easy, Lord?   He rose to go find
Caleb.

Chapter 9

Caleb stared at the name, then at Doug. "Who again gave you this name?"

"An instructor from college. She taught suspect identification and was one of the best teaching that in the country. She's written books and lectured all over the place. Betty James."

"I've heard of her. In fact, I've taken some of her online courses. She is good." Caleb looked at the name again. "You haven't done anything with it yet?"

Doug shook his head. "I figured you'd want to pass it on to the task force and let them run it. If we can keep her name out of it for now, that would be appreciated."

"That we can do. How's Darcy?"

"I saw her earlier today. She's scared, terrified the word coming to mind. I'm not how we're going to get through to her, that she needs to take precautions, more than she is at any rate."

"She's independent, Doug, and doesn't want to give up any freedom. Bill really wants her to come work for him."

Doug shook his head. "I doubt that will happen." He stood. "If there's nothing else, I'm headed for Mac's. He asked me to stop by today."

"I'll find you if I need to."

Doug headed for his uncle's office in the cafe. Mac had asked him to find him there when he could. He tapped at the door, looked in and then back down the hallway. Mac must be out in the cafe, he thought. He seated himself in one of the chairs Mac kept in there.

Mac stopped before he reached the door and watched his nephew. He nodded. Doug was hurting and it wasn't just from the terror that was being thrust at them. It was Darcy, he suspected, and how was he to help Doug? Lord, give me the words I need.

Doug looked up and greeted his uncle, surprised that Mac took the chair beside him.

"Talk to me, Doug. You're hurting. Tell your uncle what's wrong."

Doug shook his head. "I just don't know how you do it, Mac. You read people so well." He sighed, then looked down at the floor. "It's everything, I guess. We've been through so much over the last years with friends and family. Now this with the emergency services."

Mac nodded, his eyes on Doug, and waited. When Doug didn't continue and won't look at him, Mac spoke. "It's more than that, Doug. You hide so much under your jokes, teasing and laughter. You're hurting in your heart."

"I am, Mac. I made a very foolish choice years ago, thinking I was making the best decision. It wasn't. I hurt someone very badly, and now I don't know how to make it right."

"Darcy." At Doug's nod, he spoke openly with him. "You likely thought you were being noble, walking away from her. Don't say anything. You didn't have to, I could tell something was different. You just stopped talking about her. Now, she's here in your town, and you realized what a fool you were." Doug's eyes shot to his uncle's at that. "That's what you were, Doug, young and foolish. Now, what are you going to do about it?"

Doug shrugged, eyes going to the floor. "She's not backing down from me this time. She's telling me exactly how she feels and how she felt when I left. And she's right. I should have talked to her."

Mac shook his head. What a mess, Lord. "Darcy hasn't told you to stay away from her, to leave her totally alone, that she doesn't want to see you again?" Again Doug shook his head. "Then there's hope for you yet. To use an old-fashioned term, court her. Get to know her again."

Doug's eyes thoughtfully regarded his uncle. "So, how does this courting work?"

"Flowers, candy or fruit if she prefers, walks, dinners, quiet conversations. Be there for her when she needs someone. Anticipate her wishes. Go that extra mile. Just be her friend. Let her see your heart. I can tell she's been hurt by life and is questioning why and how God could allow it to happen. Pray for her. Don't push her towards God. He has to draw her." Mac paused, trying to find the words he wanted to say what he needed to say. "When I think of all you kids over the years, the picture of a lion always comes up for you, Doug. You have the heart that wants to serve, to protect, to love. You have some of that, but you are missing that one piece that would make you whole. Darcy's it. Treat her with care, my boy. Bring the strong heart of a lion into play. You'll figure it out."

"Thanks, Mac. I needed this talk." He grinned at his uncle. "You always have a verse for us during times like this. What's mine?"

Mac shook his head. "You kids." He stopped to think. "I'll come up with the right one for you. It's just not there yet."

"Thanks, Mac." Doug stood, laid his hand on his uncle's shoulder, then walked away, deep in thought. So just how did he manage to court Darcy, as his uncle put it? That would be the challenge. He groaned as his phone dinged with a text message. He pulled it out and then headed back to the office. These days were getting longer and longer.

Darcy watched as Doug walked rapidly back to the department building, then turned her eyes to the cafe. She turned as a customer spoke to her. At the end of the day, she was exhausted. Sorting through her paperwork, she stuck what she needed to do at home into her briefcase and locking up, headed home. As she approached her home, her steps slowed. Something was off. She walked slower and stopped at the front walk. A parcel sat on the steps. She wasn't expecting any deliveries to her home, they all went to her shop. Sighing, she pulled out her phone to make that call she always hated to make. Now it would get out where she was living.

Frankie Brennan approached her as she sat on the curb, arms curled around her knees. She looked up at him, squinting against the setting sun. Frankie stood, staring down at her, an inscrutable look on his face, then he reached out to help her stand.

"So, tell me, what was it this time?"

"This time?" Frank turned puzzled eyes on her. "You've had other packages and haven't called us."

She shook her head. "Not in this town. I've moved a couple of times recently, and somehow, each time he's found me. Talk to Caleb. He has the name." She turned to stare at her house. "What did you find?"

"Do you really want to know?"

She turned her eyes back to Frankie. "Nothing surprises me, Frankie, not any more. I worked as a forensics psychologist."

He took a quick look at her, then turned his attention to the crime scene team packing up. "Black roses, dead at that. And a note." He handed her the evidence bag.

She read it and nodded. "It's the same guy. How did he find me? I have been so careful."

"The man you mentioned - law enforcement?" At her nod, he continued, "That could be how he's finding you."

"He's off the force, so shouldn't have access to any sites where he could track me down. I've kept out of the media in the last five years, trying just to disappear completely."

"I'll walk through your house for you. Officers have searched outside looking for evidence but it looks like he walked up the concrete so there were no traces of him."

"Of course there wouldn't be. There never were."

Frankie shared a look with Doug, who had come up behind her. Doug shook his head at Frankie.

"If there's nothing else, Darcy, let me into your home and I'll check it out for you." He smiled at her. "There's no sign he got in."

She opened the door and turned off the security system for him, then turned, seeing Doug standing on the city walk for the first time. She walked back to him.

"How long have you been here?"

"Not long. Mom finally called me to let me know you had police all over your place and just where was I? She's taken with you, you know."

"Your mom's a sweet lady, Doug. She shouldn't be getting mixed up with this. It seems that my stalker or assailant or whatever name you want to give him has found me once again."

Doug looked up as Frankie approached them.

"Your house is clear, Darcy. We'll let you know what we find out about the package."

She snorted, surprising the two men. "You won't find out anything. The flowers will have been bought about a week ago, in some town far from here, and the packing is something you can pick up at any department store. The note: that's just his scare tactics that no longer work."

Doug looked at Frankie. He hadn't heard about the note.

"We need to take that note seriously. We'll have to contact the other police department to get their file."

She threw up her hands. "Sure. Of course, you will. I might as well take out a bill board and announce to the world where I'm living." She turned to storm away but stopped as Doug laid a hand on her arm.

"Easy, Darcy, don't bite at Frankie. He's doing his job, which you well know. Work with us, not against us."

She turned eyes on him that were dark with emotion. "Just what do you know about something like this, Doug? I worked with it, and now I'm living it."

Doug nodded. "We get that, Darcy. All I'm saying is that we want to help you. We're not that other force you think let you down. We want to solve this so you don't have to walk around in fear any more."

Frankie spoke up. "Doug's right, Darcy. We do want to solve this. I'll get back to you on this." He walked away to where a patrol officer was waiting for him.

Doug turned Darcy back to her house, picking up her briefcase and carrying it for her. "Come, let's get you into your home."

"Doug, you don't have to do this."

"Yes, I do." He grinned down at her, teasing sparkling in his eyes. "Mac told me I had to."

She shook her head at that, then sighed. "I hate this, Doug. I thought I had my freedom back. Now I'll be looking over my shoulder everywhere I go, studying strangers to see if one of them is him."

Doug watched the emotions playing across her face. Lord, she's hurting so much. How can I reach through all that to her heart again? He grinned. "Well, Darcy, we could always start dating again. I'd be there for you."

She stared at him, mouth open until he reached with a lean finger and tapped it close. "You and me? Dating again? Where did that come from?"

"From twelve years ago, Darcy. I don't know if I can ever make you understand how sorry I am. Will you at least consider being my friend?"

She finally nodded. "Friends. And only friends."

We'll see, Darcy, Doug thought. "Mom has dinner ready if you're interested. If not, let me take you out somewhere."

"You mean, starting tonight? Doug, what are you thinking?"

"I'm thinking that I am looking at a very beautiful lady that I want to spend time with, whose friendship I've missed a lot."

He watched from the onlookers from across the road. He had shaken her, he could tell. Good, he thought. Then his mind turned to other thoughts and he walked away, plotting his next plan of terror.

Chapter 10

Frankie tracked Caleb down in his office.

"What do you know about Darcy O'Shaughnessy?"

"Why do you ask about her?" Caleb was cautious, not willing to give even Frankie information on her.

"She had an interesting parcel left on her front step today." Frankie handed Caleb photos and a copy of the note. "She didn't say much, other than to indicate she was the victim of someone and that he had found her. When I contacted the department in Reeceton, they asked how she was, wanted her contact information, and told me they had been trying to get in touch with her. They had new information on the man stalking her."

Caleb shook his head. "She won't talk with them. They're the reason she's on the run. See if they'll give you the information. If not, we'll set something up here with only one of their officers coming over."

"They can track her down, knowing where she's living now."

"They can, but they won't. I'll talk to the chief over there and make sure it doesn't happen. It was one of their officers who caused all this in the first place." Caleb briefly told Frankie what had transpired.

"It's no wonder she said what she did. Doug was going to see if he could talk to her. Now that's an interesting couple."

Caleb smiled at Frankie. "You picked up on that too? Dave says he thinks she's the lady Doug walked away from in college."

Frankie nodded. "Yep, that would be her. There are sparks there when the two are together, and they're trying their best to not let anyone know."

"She's hurting, Frankie. Doug has mentioned that she doesn't seem to put much stock in her faith any more."

"We'll pray her back, Caleb. Any more word from the task force?"

"They're running with the ideas that Darcy passed on." At Frankie's look of surprise, Caleb grinned. "She met with Bill and I completely confidentially so don't say anything. He's just saying he spoke with her and is passing on her thoughts. Every other department around her thinks she got a very raw deal by the way. He says they've been able to eliminate a lot of paperwork they still hadn't had a chance to get through. He wants her to go work for him when this is all over."

Frank stood, thought about that, then shook his head. "No, I can't see that happening. She's burnt out that way and sees really happy in her shop and online store from what I'm hearing about town." He froze as his phone dinged.

"Another one, Caleb, this time the police again."

"Where?"

"Greentown again."

"How many?"

"None. They found the package in time. Another bomb, aimed at the bomb squad."

"I want this guy and want him before he hits us. He hasn't hit us yet and that makes me wonder what he's planning." Caleb turned to his phone as Frankie nodded and left.

Doug watched as Darcy paced through her home, not saying anything, but keeping his eyes on her. He finally moved into a spot where she would have to walk right into him. Hands on her shoulders, he kept her in place.

"Darcy, talk to me."

She shook her head. "Talking never works."

"Maybe it didn't with some you've talked to. It will with me. It always did." He reached and drew her into a hug.

Darcy stiffened as she felt Doug's arms around her. She hadn't let anyone this close to her in years, not her parents, not her sister or brother. She couldn't remember the last time she had been hugged. Then it came to her. Doug's was the last one she could remember. She relaxed suddenly, hugging him back, and burrowing her head into his chest.

He stood, not fully comprehending that she had accepted his hug. His arms tightened around her as he sought to make her understand just how much he wanted to protect her. She was just tall enough that his chin rested comfortably on her head.

"Thank you, Doug. I haven't had a hug in years."

"You're welcome, Darcy. When you're ready to really talk, I'm really ready to listen to you."

She leaned back to look up at him. "Thank you, Doug. At some point, I guess I should, but I just don't know. Aren't you on call tonight?"

He shook his head. "Not tonight. So can I ask a friend out to dinner?"

She frowned at him, then nodded. "Sure why not. But is there another restaurant in town?"

He laughed as he let her go. "There is. Go. Get yourself ready." He watched as she walked away from him and prayed that he could reach her heart, but that God would reach it first. He could see a softening in her.

Darcy stopped in the entry to her living room. Doug stood looking out the front window, stance relaxed but she could see the intensity that she knew he was capable of. He was still on guard, on watch.

"Doug." Her voice was quiet as she spoke, but he turned instantly, a smile in place and he came towards her.

"All set? I made reservations at the Italian place. Hope that's okay."

She nodded. "That's fine. Just let me lock up."

He stood and watched as Doug helped Darcy into his truck, then drove away. He turned to follow, not seeing the neighbour watching him intently, then heading indoors to make a call. He had been seen and now the ones he was after would be after him. He stared around as he drove, trying to find the best place to stage the ambush he was planning. He giggled to himself. It would be the best and the biggest of them all. He would stage it so that they had to bring in help from outside of town. That would make it so much better. He would stage it and be gone before the time was set for it to

happen. Soon, he thought, soon would be
the time.

Chapter 11

Doug watched as emotions skittered across Darcy's face. She sat relaxed in her chair, but he knew she was on edge. There was a fine tightness in her words that shouldn't be there.

"How are your parents and your brother and sister?"

She turned her gaze back to him and shrugged. "My parents no longer speak to me, nor do my siblings. They in fact moved far away from me. They all blame me for what happened."

"Oh, Darcy. I'm sorry."

She shrugged. "It's life. That's what happens. Let's move on to another topic."

Doug went to speak and stopped. "No, just let me say something without interrupting. Are you sure they blame you or where they threatened too?"

She looked up at him, shock on her face. "I never thought of that, to tell you the truth. With the words they levelled at me, I don't think that's the case."

"As part of the investigation to the parcel on your stop, Frankie will have to contact them. It's just routine. I can fill him in for you on what you've just said."

She stopped him. "Go ahead. I'm sure he'll get an earful from them all too. Now that you've persuaded me to come eat with you, isn't it time we ordered?"

"That we can, sweetheart. Here's comes Carrie, our waitress, now." He hadn't meant for that to slip our. Or maybe he did. That's what she was to him.

She ignored what he called her. Likely just a slip of the tongue, she thought.

The meal over, he tucked her back into his vehicle, then stopped, staring around. He turned slowly in a circle, trying to find the body the eyes he could on him belonged to. There was no one he could see.

Darcy watched him, eyes narrowing. Yes, Doug could feel it too.

"You feel them too, don't you?"

Doug nodded. "That's what you're feeling all the time?" At her nod, he continued, "You need to be very careful.

This guy is good. He's hiding somewhere we can't see him, but he can see us."

"So which one is it? The guy after you or the one after me?" Her voice slowed. "Doug, I need to talk to Caleb and Bill. I have just had a horrible thought."

"Tonight?" At her nod, he was on the phone with Caleb, making arrangements to meet in his office. "Caleb will set up a conference call with Bill."

Darcy sat, her body tense, in Caleb's office waiting for the conference call to come through. She didn't like what she had to say, and she knew they would like it even less. Lord, You and I haven't been talking much lately. I could sure use Your help right now. She felt a peace begin to move through her, making sure she was doing the right thing.

Caleb saw the slight release in her body and wondered just as the call came in from Bill.

"We're all here, Bill. Darcy asked for this call, so I'll let her talk."

"Good evening, Darcy. What do you have for us?"

"I'm not sure if I have any new or not. I had a thought about our guy and my guy. What if they're one and the same?" She heard Bill's quick intake of breath and saw Caleb and Doug both start with shock. "There could be two guys, but the way things are playing out, it just doesn't make sense. The sergeant that's after me, I looked into his background when it all started. He's lied about it, lied about his schooling, provided false documents. Check with his commanding officer. I turned copies of everything over to him.

"I had forgotten, or rather tried to forget, that this was false and that what I gave you for this emergency service stalker is almost word for word for what I dug up about him. I know what people will say. You don't have to say it. They'll say I'm providing this so you'll catch my stalker. Not happening. I want to see justice done for what's going on now."

Bill was quick to speak. "I have already spoken with his commanding officer, and you have confirmed what he said. They went back over his life with a fine tooth comb and tracked down all the lies and the truth. That's one of the reasons they're trying to get in touch with you.

"Now about that. I agree with you. From what we've been digging up in our investigations, we tracing it back to someone just like you described to me. We have a number of possibilities, but he's top of the list. Why would he be going to this extent?"

"Because to him I represent another failure. I exposed him for what he is, and he can't handle that. Also, he wants revenge against the law enforcement group. He has set his sights on those personnel and expanded it as his mind deteriorates to include any emergency service personnel." She watched as Doug left to take a call. Caleb's eyes were steady on her and he nodded for her to continue. "He will continue to escalate, Bill, unless you catch him." She continued to describe what she was feeling and thinking and what she expected to happen. "I hope I'm wrong, but knowing this fellow, I don't think I am. He's like a chameleon, he can change appearances and appear to be destitute or to be a millionaire and anyone in between.

One thing he can't hide are the effects his alcoholism have had on him. He always drank and I suspect even more so now."

She stopped and stared at Caleb in horror. "It was him that day." She choked on her words as Caleb rose to come towards her.

"Who, Darcy?"

"That man I stepped into outside my shop. It was him. That's why he seemed so familiar. And he was in my shop a couple of days later." She began to shake. "He's found me."

"Caleb, what's happening?" Bill voice came through the phone.

Caleb filled him in on what had happened.

"I don't like this, Caleb, not one bit. He's found her, knows her shop, and now by the sounds of it knows her home."

"I agree. She had a parcel left for her today, and the note would indicate that."

"Parcel?"

"A parcel with dead roses and a note. Frankie sent them on to the lab."

"I don't like that. Listen, I have to go. I have a meeting with the task force leaders in about 15 minutes. I'm passing on this information. Darcy, I have to let them know where you are now. It's become common knowledge if he's found you."

She nodded, then said, "I know. I hate this, Bill. I have finally felt safe after all these years. Doug mentioned that this guy may have threatened my family. I haven't spoken to any of them in years. Talk to them and find out if that's what happened."

"We'll do that, Darcy, and in such a way they won't know why. Take care of all of your guys, Caleb."

Caleb reached to hang up the phone, then turned back to Darcy, leaning against the edge of his desk, hands on the desk top.

"So what now, Caleb?"

"Now? We work at keeping you safe. Doug will be back shortly, I suspect, and take you home. Frankie says you have good security at your shop and your home. But you can't lock up your shop during the day and stay safe that way. What I would suggest is that I find one of our lady officers, who would like to come work with you, and work undercover for now. Would you agree with that?"

She nodded. "I know I have to have help. I just hate putting the customers in the way."

Caleb nodded, "It's like that for any of the businesses right now in any of the towns. No one knows who will be safe or not. We're getting stopped all the time on the street, being asked that very question. We'll keep you out of it."

She rose and headed for the door. "You'll try, Caleb, but it only takes one person with loose lips to let the secret out."

"We'll do our best, Darcy." Caleb hesitated to meddle but felt he should say something. "Darcy." He waited for her to turn but she didn't. He sighed. No, she wasn't making it easy for him. "Darcy, let Doug help you. He's never said and I'm only guessing, but you're the one he has never been able to forget and move on from, aren't you?"

She finally nodded, turning back to face him, fighting to keep the tears from falling. "He's mine, too, Caleb. I just can't move on and I want too."

Caleb reached into his pocket and pulled out his handkerchief, holding it out to her.

She took it, staring first at it and at him. He grinned. "My mother brought me up to carry one. Hannah thinks it's a really good idea, and she's been teaching our boys to have one on hand for damsels in distress. Many of my friends, the ones that are married, engaged or would like to be, are now carrying handkerchiefs. They like the idea of giving their ladies something substantial, more than a piece of paper."

She shook her head at him, a bit of smile peeking through. "Your Mom raised you well." She handed him back the handkerchief. "Here, you'll need it for your lady. I'm fine."

"No, I don't think you are. You're thinking of running again, and I can tell you, that won't work. Doug wants to start over with you. I think he's already talked to you about that. Give him a chance. Better still, give God another chance. He has never ever turned His back on you."

"It feels like He has, Caleb, so where is He?"

"He's the same one He always has been, the same yesterday, today and tomorrow. He also says in Jeremiah that He alone knows the plans and purposes He has for you and that they're for your good."

She shook her head a bit slower this time. "I'll think about it. You find this guy and get that off my back, it will change."

Caleb shook his head this time. "Doesn't work that way. You can't bargain with God."

She turned and headed for the door. "Just find this guy, Caleb. None of us can go on like this."

She almost ran Doug down as she left the office. Doug's eyes sought Caleb's, then looked down at her.

"Ready to go home?"

She nodded. "More than ready. I have to be at the store early tomorrow for a delivery, and I already know I'm not going to get enough sleep."

Chapter 12

Darcy looked up the next morning as the doorbell tinkled and a young woman, around her age, she thought, walked in.

"Hi, I'm looking for Darcy." Her voice was low and well-modulated but Darcy could see she was missing nothing as she looked around.

"I'm Darcy. How may I help you?"

"I was told you were looking for a sales clerk who liked arts and crafts and that kind of objects. Here's a letter of reference. Do you mind if I look around while you read it?"

Darcy shook her head as she took the letter. "No, go ahead." She turned back to the counter and opened the letter. As she suspected, it was from Caleb, recommending Abby Lucas for a job. Well, Abby Lucas, let's see if you will fit. Caleb says you're an excellent officer and a more than excellent shot.

"So, you're Abby Lucas?" Darcy walked towards her, hand outstretched.

"You come highly recommended. Have you ever worked retail before?"

Abby nodded. "I worked during high school and for a while afterwards until I decided what I wanted to do. I miss it." She turned in a circle, face alight. "I love this place. I recognize a lot of the names."

"I have drawn in quite a few artisans. Did you know there's an online store as well that is really taking off?"

Abby shook her head, and then the two women were lost in talk of the store, the online store and where Darcy would like to see the store go.

Customers came and went, greeting both women, Abby in particular. She would just grin at the comments from those she knew and say nothing, other than that she needed to fill in some of her spare time.

"It's lunch time, Abby. I usually close up for an hour or so if I can. Come on. Mac's is just down the road, or we can go to the deli and grab something."

"Mac's works. He does a great broasted chicken salad."

"And why have I never been told that? Mac usually decides for me."

Abby laughed at that. "He will if you let him but don't let him. I should tell you, he's my uncle on my Dad's side."

Darcy's hands flew into the air. "Why doesn't that surprise me?"

"What should surprise you?" A deep voice behind her caused her to jump and scream.

She spun to face Doug as Abby laughed beside her. A grin on his face, Doug faced her, Dave standing beside him.

"Hi, Abby. What are you doing here? Shouldn't you be working?"

"Shut up, Doug. Come on, Dave, let's head in before Mac's is completely full."

Darcy watched them walk away, then turned back to Doug. "Abby's working for me now."

"She is." Doug's eyes never left her face until he turned her back to the cafe. "Now I know what Caleb was up to."

They were seated before she could come up with a reply. Laughter filled their mealtime. Darcy couldn't remember the last time she had had such a fun meal, out with friends. Dave and Doug seemed to be doing their best to keep the two ladies entertained.

Later that day, Darcy had just gotten home and kicked off her shoes when the doorbell rang. Looking out, she pulled the door open.

"Didn't I just see you?"

"You did.   Can I come in for a minute?"

Doug was acting strange, she thought, as she nodded, keeping one hand behind his back. As the door closed, he turned, then brought out a sheaf of beautiful yellow roses, the ones he remembered she loved.

"Doug, what did you do? Buy out the florist?"

He shook his head. "Almost but not quite. You need flowers, Darcy."

"Doug!" She turned to head for the kitchen. "Come on back while I put these into water. What are you apologizing for?"

"Darcy, you wound me. I'm not apologizing. I'm done with that." He pointed at the flowers. "Those flowers are for a lady I happen to think a lot of and would like to spend more time with."

She stopped, staring up at him. "Brew us some coffee while I go change. Then you can catch me up on what's happening."

He sighed, knowing he had just blown his chance, and turned to find what he needed to make the coffee.

Darcy slowly shut her door and leaned back against it. Had he really said that, knowing what was going on with her, the danger she was in? Then she shrugged. He faced danger head on every day, so what she was facing was likely nothing. She slowly walked to her closet to hang up the clothes she had on and pick out something else. Tonight, she needed comfort clothes and reached for her old worn sweat pants and a favourite T-shirt.

She stopped in the kitchen doorway, watching as he stood looking out the window over the sink, the sun hi-lighting his body. He is so good looking, she thought. I was always the envy of my friends. She padded softly across the floor and reached to hug him. He turned, surprise in his movements and then he hugged her back.

"What's that for?"

He felt her shrug. "Just because." He could barely hear the words. "I missed your hugs, Doug."

His arms tightened around her. He hadn't blown it after all. He felt his phone vibrate and ignored it.

She stepped back and looked up at him, suspicious dampness in her eyes. "You need to answer that. I'll get our coffee."

Doug growled in frustration at the interruption until he heard Caleb's words. The man had struck again, this time a satellite court in Oak City, killing a justice of the peace, a court reporter and a public defender. Where would it stop, Lord? Lead us to him.

Darcy turned from her gardens as Doug found her, taking the cup she offered him. His hand found hers and he was trying hard not to cling to it. She drew him off to a bench at the side of the garden and pulled him down.

"Bad news?"

Doug nodded. "And three more deaths. This guy just doesn't care."

"No, he never has and never will. He needs to be stopped. How do you do that?"

Doug shook his head. "The task force is working on that but haven't compiled enough information to know how to attract him into a trap."

"I know how to do that, but you won't like it."

He turned his head and read her face. "No, I don't like it. Please don't offer yourself as bait. I just found you again. My heart won't take losing you again. Darcy, please let me speak without interrupting." His eyes never left hers. "I can't make up for how I hurt you or the years we have lost. All I can say is that as a young and foolish man, I thought I was doing the right thing, and I didn't. I hurt the woman I love more than life itself in a way she should never have been hurt. And if this woman will consent to try again, it would feel me with delight. Will you consider my suit?"

"Your suit?" She giggled. "Sorry, it sounds like I'm supposed to approve of your dress." At his glare, she sobered. "Someone has been talking old fashioned living to you, haven't they? And I would hazard a guess the first initial is "M". I have thought about it a lot since we ran into each other in the cafe that day, and through all the words we spoken and not spoken. I'm not the same person I was twelve years ago, Doug. I am not the same person I would have been had we married back then. I think you actually did both of us a favour by walking away. Neither of us was ready to marry, to start a family at that age. We had not experienced life as we should have. Now we have. Now we have been drawn back together as we are supposed to be."

She stared away across the yard, Doug watching the emotions playing across her face. She reached out her hand. "Where's the handkerchief you guys all carry?"

He stared at her as he reached for his pocket. "Who told you that?"

"A very tall, good looking, very married police chief who was raised right and who is influencing his friends."

Bless you, Caleb. Whatever you said to her last night got through.

"But what about God, Darcy? Where is He in your life?"

She sighed. "He's been after me all these years, Doug. Caleb was right. He never moved, I did. I just need to find the steps back."

"One step, Darcy, and you've already taken that."

She nodded, then laid her head on his shoulder. "Where do we go from here, Doug?"

He wrapped his arm around her. "Only where you want to, Darcy. I was told to go slow and court you, Darcy. I think that sounds like good advice and a lot of fun." He sighed as his phone dinged again.

"Is this what your life is like?"

"Not usually this bad, Darcy, but with this guy out there, it's going crazy." His voice died away as he read his message.

"Who'd he hit, Doug?"

"The training academy. No casualties but the building is a total loss."

She straightened up. "He hit the building at this time of night, knowing no one would be there. Was there any notice given?"

"Let me ask." He read the response, then turned to her, questions in his eyes. "There was. How did you know?"

"He's changing tactics. He's not getting the attention in the media that he wants. So now, he'll be leaving a note, targeting a certain group or a building or even a school, heaven forbid. Once it gets out that there's a target, you'll have media all over the place, speculating on how it is and why he hasn't been caught yet and how many times has he already hit. The media's already connecting the dots and asking the hard questions. Those questions are driving him to change and adapt. Then he'll go silent and you won't have a clue where the next target will be." She looked up, fear in her face. "I think the last and biggest target will be here, if you don't catch him first."

Doug pulled her to her feet and into her house. "Grab what you need for the night. We're heading back to the office. We're going to need to meet with Caleb and Bill, and I think it's time you came out of hiding and met with the task force. They're getting what you're saying second hand. They need to hear it from you."

He stood in the darkness and watched as Doug tucked her into his truck and drove away once again. Where were they headed this time, he wondered? Soon, he would have her in his clutches and make her pay for what she had put him through. The voices told him that. He clutched his head and fell to his knees as the voices clamoured in his head, each voice trying to drown out the other. If he succeeded with what he was to do, would they leave him alone?

Chapter 13

Caleb slowly hung up his phone and sighed before turning to Doug and Darcy seated across from him. Frankie stood in front of the closed door.

"Bill agrees with Doug, Darcy. He feels it's time you came out of hiding as well and talked at least to the task force leaders. I'm sorry. We've tried."

She nodded. "I know you have and I appreciate that. Get Bill to set up a meeting with only the leaders and on a neutral base. Here would be nice, but perhaps Oak City would be better." She looked at the men in the room with her. "It needs to be done. It wouldn't have mattered if we had done it earlier, he still would have been hitting targets. Now, do you have an office and a computer I can work from?"

Doug pulled her to her feet and led her away. "You can use mine. Do you need access to anything?"

She shook her head. "No, I kept all my credentials up to date for some reason. I guess this is it." She settled into his desk chair. "I'm not taking this away from you, am I?"

"No, I can use Tom's if I need to. Can I get you anything?"

"Some juice would be nice. Thank you." She had dismissed him, her thoughts already on the man who was terrorizing her and the town around.

Frankie stopped Doug in the hallway. "Is she really okay with this?"

Doug shrugged. "I'm not sure that she is but she has to for herself to move forward. Any more attacks?"

Frankie shook his head. "It's like what she said. He's gone silent for a space. I'm expecting to hear of another attack." He groaned as his phone dinged. "And I'm right."

"Where did he hit?"

"The fire department in the county, the volunteer one. All their equipment is gone. No one was there at the time."

"I wish we could catch him. He just keeps going and going. What's the word on his background?"

"I don't know how your lady does it, but she read him well. What she told us is about what we're finding. There are still lots of blanks to fill in but it's an interesting read. He really lied about himself and provided false documents to get on the police. Whoever did the background check on him has a lot of explaining to do."

"Find out who it was and check their bank balance from when he joined the force. It might be an interesting read."

"Those are my thoughts and I have a team working on that."

Darcy stared at the computer screen and shuddered. This was one of the reasons she had walked away. She couldn't handle the senseless violence any more. This guy was sick.

She looked down at the notes she was taking, then at the clock. She needed to get up and move around. Sometimes, pacing helped.

She opened the office door, and Doug looked up from where he was sitting, hard at his paperwork. He rose and came to stand in front of her.

"You okay?"

She shook her head. "I just need a break and to walk. Is there somewhere I can walk in safety?"

"There is. Get your sweater and I'll lock my office door. No one will go in. What you're working on will be safe for now."

He led her out the back door and reached for her hand. She relished the feel of strength and safety communicated through his touch. After a few rounds of the parking lot, he could feel the tenseness dissipating from her.

"Want to talk about it?"

She shrugged. "This guy is really sick, Doug. I had no idea how bad when he came after me." She paused in her steps, thought and then moved forward. "I'm trying to make sense of it all before I talk to the task force. When is that set up for?"

"For tomorrow, today actually, 10:00 a.m. We'll need to leave here by 7:30 so I can get you there in time. It's about a two-hour drive."

"You're taking me?"

He nodded. "Caleb and I. We're planning to disguise you, though."

"As what?"

"That's the surprise. We're still getting everything we need. Will Abby be okay at the store?"

"Abby. I forgot. She won't be needed if I'm not there."

"Oh, I think she will be. She told me she loves the store, more than the police. Don't be surprised if she approaches you to work for you full time."

"That would be wonderful but I don't want to take one of Caleb's people from him,"

"You won't be. She's already been talking to me about finding something else. She's getting married in a few months and she and her fiance would like her to make a career change. The store is just up her alley. She has always had a desire to work with the arts."

"Then get keys and the codes to her and she can work today."

Doug drew Darcy into a quiet, dim corner of the yard. His arms around her, he just stood, letting her relax against him.

"Thank you, Doug. That means a lot."

"Thought it would. Now we need to go back to work." He stood staring down at her, her face barely visible in the lighting.

She looked at him, then shook her head. "Not here, Doug."

He nodded, then led her back to the door, letting her back into his office. "What can I get you?"

"Maybe some coffee this time. I need the caffeine to stay anyway."

Caleb found him in the break room where he stood, head down, fatigue in every movement. He watched Doug, knowing he couldn't give much more that day, and it was still way too early in the day. They had to get Darcy to Oak City and back safely, get her through the meeting, and then decompress her on the way home.

"Doug."

Doug roused from his reverie and shook his head. "Caleb. What's the word?"

"We're set for the task force meeting. We're not meeting at the police department. Bill and I decided we needed somewhere else that Darcy wouldn't be seen and known."

"So, where are we meeting?" They went on to discuss the meeting site and what they had found out.

"Is she ready?" Caleb turned to look back through the door.

"About as ready as she will be. We took a walk out in the yard a while ago so she could clear her head. She's sorting through the facts and what-ifs and innuendos. She was always good at that in college. She can see right through shams and lies." He stopped, then turned to Caleb. "I think that's why that sergeant is after her so much. He knows she's likely spoken out against him, and if he can get rid of her, then the talk will die down. At least that's what I figure he thinks."

"That's what we're all thinking. It's going to be quite the task to keep her safe once she goes public. Somewhere along the line it will come out that she's back and helping on this."

Doug nodded, then moved to pour the coffee. "And she knows that and dreads that. Do we have somewhere we can put her if we need to?"

"Where do we always put them? I spoke with Abe Finlay at Rebel's security. He's willing to put security in place for her. Now that they're doing strictly training and not away, he has guys he can pull off that to put with her. In fact, they'll be with us today."

"His guys are good." Doug picked up the two cups of coffee. "What time do we leave?"

"I think 8 is sufficient time, seeing as it's not in Oak City."

Doug nodded, then yawned. He had not been sleeping well since the accident and pulling an all-nighter was not helping him.

Darcy looked up as Doug set her coffee cup beside her, absentmindedly thanking him. "Get some sleep, Doug. You're running on empty."

He stretched out on his couch. "I will. I spoke with Caleb. We're not meeting at the police department. They've come up with an alternative place, so we don't have to leave until about 8. And we have a friend and his team members providing security for you." He dozed off as he finished, not catching how Darcy sat back, mouth open, to stare at him.

"Just like that, he tells me that and goes to sleep."

"Tells you what?" Frankie's voice behind her caused her to jump and give a small scream.

He grinned as she spun around to confront him. "Let me know next time you're there."

"I will. Deirdre says the same thing."

"And she would be?"

"My wife."

"And in that case, I don't blame her."

"But she's scary, you know, really scary. I wouldn't want to meet her in a dark alley."

"Frankie, that's not a very nice thing to say about your wife."

He started laughing, then perched on the corner of Doug's desk as he filled Darcy in on the adventure he and Deirdre had had just before they were married.

"You really didn't tell her that, did you?"   Darcy was laughing at the descriptions Frankie was giving.

"Sure, I did.   She can pick up languages in a month, has been threatened overseas by who knows by what all or who all, stared down a youth holding a switchblade in the youth centre she used to manage, can hot wire vehicles, and picks my pockets all the time without me knowing it. You need to meet her."

"I would be honoured to, but that's not why you came in here, to talk about your wife."

He shook his head. "No, it's not. This was found on your front porch late last night, after you two had left. We have a patrol driving by and he walks the outside of the house and grounds as well."

She took the note and read it, an unreadable look on her face. She handed it back to him. "He's living up, or rather down, to what I would expect from him. Have you given this to Caleb?"

"I have and he's sent it on to the task force. This is really entwining you with what's going on."

"I know, Frankie. I'm just not seeing the connection, though. I knew him from when I did that one case only, and it was his negligence that caused the deaths, not mine. He tried to be a big hero without the knowledge to work it through and resented the fact that his superiors called in others to help."

"There has to be something more as to why he fixated on you. You had never met him before that one case?"

She started to shake her head, then stopped, eyes resting on Doug. "Now wait. No, it can't be." She turned to the computer again, fingers flying over the keyboard. She stopped, sitting back, and drawing her breath in with almost a sob. "There, Frankie. There's the connection. If you hadn't said something that triggered it, I would never have remembered."

Frankie laid his hand on her shoulder as he studied what she had brought up on the screen. "Can you print that, and send that address to my email? Here's my email address."

She nodded, fingers flying once more as she went between screens. She turned to the printer, pulling off the pages.

"Frankie, I don't think Doug remembers him at all. Have the task force start looking at every member of that group. I'll pretty much guarantee you that everyone of us targeted is in there or somehow connected to that group."

"I'm on it. You had better tell Doug, though. It's better it comes from you than someone else."

"I will." She watched Frankie close the door, then sighing, rose and walked around the desk. Perching on the side of the sofa seat, she laid her hand on Doug's shoulder and gently shook him.

Doug's eyes popped open and he was instantly alert.

"Darcy, I slept. It isn't time to go yet, is it?"

She shook her head, then stood as he sat up. He pulled her back down beside him.

"No, it's not time to go yet. Frankie just left. I had another package on my porch. But while we were talking, I remembered something. He's gone to talk to the task force leader." She leaned against him. "Do you remember that group we were part of for a while, that was set up to run what-if scenarios?"

"I do. It's been a long time since we did that." He stilled. "Why bring that up?"

"Because he was part of it at one point, until we all asked him to leave."

"I remember that. He didn't take it well. Are you saying that's what this is all about?"

"I would say part of it is. He seems to be going after anyone who has crossed him and kept him from getting ahead, even when he didn't deserve to get ahead."

Doug leaned his head back. "And we missed that."

"Who would have thought about that, Doug? We were teenagers or early 20's at that point. We all thought it was over and done with. The trouble is, he's not smart enough to think up all this by himself. Who's fueling the anger and giving the instructions?"

"One of the old faculty? One of the older students? This has just changed the focus of the group. I don't like this, Darcy."

"Nor do I. This makes you as much of a target as I am."

"I know. So how do we keep both of us safe?"

She shrugged. "I have no idea. Maybe God will work a miracle for us."

"You're talking to God again, are you?"

She nodded. "It seemed pointless to keep my anger against Him. He didn't cause the problem, just allowed it."

They both looked up as Caleb tapped, then opened the door. He entered, then shut it behind him. "We're about ready to move out. It's earlier than we planned but we want to take a circuitous route. Abe's waiting out back for us."

Chapter 14

Doug and Darcy were tucked into the back seat of an SUV. Darcy gave a jump as a man slipped in beside her, a grin crossing his face at her move.

Doug spoke. "Darcy, this is Abe beside you. He runs a security company. In the front are two of his men, Ian and Nathaniel. Where are the rest, Abe?"

"Matt and Micah are in front with Caleb. Luke, Joseph, and Murphy are behind us."

"You've got the whole crew today."

"We do. We have some very important clients to protect today."

Doug shook his head at Abe's words, then reached for Darcy's hand. "We're safe, Darcy, as safe as we can be."

"That's a promise, Darcy. We've never lost anyone yet, at least not permanently."

"Somehow, that's not reassuring."

"Well, when you're trying to protect someone and they want to run and do so, you're not protecting them. That's what I mean."

She shook her head. "That's supposed to bring comfort? Well, it isn't. You're supposed to keep them from running."

Ian broke up in laughter at that. "Darcy, you would fit right in with all of our ladies. Most of them ran at some point when we were trying to keep them safe."

"Really? I need to meet them and find out their strategy. I might be able to fine tune it."

Doug squeezed her hand. "I have no doubt you would refine it well. But that's not happening."

"No? I'm really good at running. Hiding, now that I'm working on." She laughed at his expression, then turned back to Abe. "So, tell me about all these ladies that you were supposed to protect."

Abe shook his head. "Really? You want to hear about them?"

She nodded.

"So far, we have Rachel, my brother-in-law's sister, then we have my sister, Rebecca."

"Wait a minute. Your own sister?"

Abe gave a sad look. "My own sister. Then, there was Matt's Sarah and Nathaniel's Elizabeth. We're still working on making sure the ladies in town know they shouldn't run when we have them in protective custody. Somehow, I don't think they're getting the message." He turned to her and with a sad look still on his face, said, "Given our record, today would be the day you'd run."

Nathaniel turned. "Elizabeth only ran because you kept calling her Whizz."

"I didn't start that name, you know. It was her Dad."

Nathaniel shook his head, smiling at a memory. "The look on her face was priceless when she was informed about that."

Darcy was laughing harder by now. "Not happening, Abe. My running days are over." She sobered at the memories. "I'm done with that. I just want this guy caught so that everyone can go on with their lives."

Doug caught Abe's eyes over Darcy's head and shook his head. Abe nodded, his eyes going back to Darcy. There was something more going on here then he knew about. That was par for the course. Lately, that seemed to be the way they operated, with not all the information they needed. Abe knew Doug would give him the information he needed when he could.

Ian pulled the van into the garage bay, following the one Matt was driving. Murphy pulled in beside them.

"Interesting meeting place that was set up, Doug." Abe opened his door and then stood looking around, assessing the area.

"I know. We didn't want Darcy coming into the department in Oak City. Bill Watson set this up. He's good friends with the man who owns this."

"We've been here before. We're going to walk through to make sure it's safe for you. Ian and Murphy are staying with you three."

Caleb stood by Abe and nodded. "Go ahead. With the doors down, we should be okay."

Abe was back in about twenty minutes. He stood for a minute watching Doug and Darcy talking. They've known each other for a while, Lord. Help us to keep them as safe as we can. His eyes raised to meet those of Caleb's and he nodded. Walking towards the SUV, he spoke to his team and sent them to their appointed tasks.

"Doug, I know you're highly trained and so is Caleb. Today, though, you're in our protective custody. If something comes up, let us asses it and react. You watch out for Darcy. Caleb will have your back.

"Now, as to the plan. It's a big house, but it's really open down stairs. We go in through the kitchen, into the great room, and then into the study. It's big, one of the biggest private studies I've seen. You're the first ones here, and you'll be the first ones to leave. Bill Watson is on his way up now. The others are being brought in by van so we don't have a lot of vehicles coming in and out.

"We're going to walk you in and to the study. If you need to leave for any reason, right hand to the ear. Got that?" At their nod, he continued, "If we come towards you at all, be prepared to move and move quickly. If we have to separate the two of you for your safety, we will. That's a given and no questions asked. Got that?" Again, he waited for their nods. "Okay, let's get you inside and behind the study doors."

Darcy held up her hand. "Abe, are you a Christian?" At his nod, she looked past him at Caleb, then back to Doug. "Can we pray first, before we go anywhere? Doug's been reminding me who really is in control."

Doug's eyes slid shut in a quiet thank you, Lord, Darcy's back.

Abe nodded, then turned to Caleb. "Caleb, will you?"

Caleb nodded as they bowed in prayer, asking for protection, wisdom, and a swift end to their fight. He really felt that they were in a fight to the end with this maniac and he knew only God could protect them.

Darcy wandered around the study, noting the well-worn books on the shelves, the sentimental knick-knacks. Then, she turned and jumped.

"Doug, what is that on the wall?"

He turned, then grinned. "Our host is a hunter. Doesn't go overseas, only hunts what is allowed."

She shuddered. "But does he have to display these things?" She pointed at the various animal heads and stuffed animals that were displayed. "I don't know if I can work in somewhere where I have dead animals staring at me. Particularly that black thing."

"That's a bear, Darcy."

"I know it is. I just didn't want to offend it by calling it by its name."

Doug swung an arm around her shoulder and turned her back to face the other end. "If you stand this way, which is how they have it set up, you won't see them."

"No, I'll just have them staring at my back. Do I have a bull's eye on it?"

Doug laughed even harder. "Darcy, I have so missed your sense of humour."

"Why? I stole it from you, if you would only remember."

Bill Watson stood in the doorway, watching them intently, then shook his head. Caleb was right. There was something going on again with those two.

"All set, Darcy?" He asked as he walked towards them.

"I would be if we could meet without those things staring at me."

"Those things? What might they be?"

She pointed over her shoulder. "Those things on the wall. They give me the creeps."

Bill laughed as Doug joined in. "I will be sure to tell the homeowner you didn't appreciate his artwork."

She looked at him, horrified. "You wouldn't, would you?"

He nodded. "And he will laugh harder that your boyfriend here is."

"He's not the boyfriend, Bill. Why does everyone think that?"

Doug and Bill exchanged amused glances, then followed her as she walked towards the table. She laid out the paperwork she had gathered and had had copied for all the leaders.

"This is hard, Bill, knowing that it still comes back to me and Doug."

"I know, Darcy. Walk us through what you have. No one here will judge you. I've already warned each and every one of them that I pull you off and send you into protective custody if that happens. Your task with us will be done at that point. And they know we can't have that. For some reason, he's decided to focus on you."

"We know why, Bill. Have you given any thought to who might be behind it all?"

Bill perched on the edge of the table, crossed his arms, and studied her. "Why do you say that?"

"I know this guy. He doesn't have the smarts to come up with this on his own. For him to have gotten where he did on the force, someone had to be behind it. There is no way he would have made it on his own."

Bill looked behind him as the task force leaders filtered in and found seats. "We're looking into that. If either one of you have names, let me know."

"There is one person who might be able to help you. All I can remember is that her first name was Emma. She's one of the smartest women I know. She was in our group for a couple of months, and then left."

"We'll try finding her and seeing if she has any input."

"That would be good. I just can't remember her last name."

Chapter 15

Abe shut the SUV door as he settled into his seat again. It had been a long day, and he wasn't sure if anything had been accomplished. At times, he had heard raised voices from the study.

Doug's arm around her, Darcy settled into her seat. It had been a brutal day, she thought, one of the worst days she had ever put in on this kind of task. Word was now out, and she no longer felt safe. Would she ever feel safe again? She doubted that.

The task force has spent hours pouring over the material, asking questions, making plans, but all that meant little as they had no idea where he was or who was behind him.

Doug pulled out his phone at a text message and read it, grim lines forming on his face again.

Darcy felt him tense. "Where this time, Doug?"

"Oak City's police department. No one was hurt but there is some damage.

Somehow, he figured out we were taking you there today. How?"

Abe's eyes shot to his, and then behind him as chatter came over his radio. "We've got company, people. Let's move, Ian."

Ian nodded. Now, this is where they excelled, protecting their people.

Three hours later, Darcy stood in her kitchen, Doug behind her. "Did we really just go through an almost demo derby?"

He laughed at her description, but nodded. "We did. Abe and his men are good. I've known him all my life and trust him completely."

Darcy turned, fatigue in her movements. "So, now what, Doug? Did we even make any progress today?"

He nodded. "We did. We eliminated suspects and now know who we are looking for. We just need to find the one behind him."

She stared at him, then moved past him towards her home office. He followed and watched as she sorted through books on her shelves.

"Do you still have your college yearbooks?"

"What?"   He was puzzled at her question.

"Our yearbooks.   Do you still have yours? I thought I had mine, but I don't see them.   In fact, I am sure I had them in my last house, but they're not here now.   I always put them in the same place."

Doug thought. "I don't at my place, but Mom might have packed them away. Lock the door after me. I'll be right back."

Doug was back almost before she had missed him, yearbooks in hand.   She reached for their junior year one and sank to the chair in the office.

"What are you looking for, Darcy?"

"I'm not sure, Doug, but something's been perplexing me all day. I won't sleep until I track it down."

"How can I help?"

"Coffee, lots of coffee."

"And some food.   You didn't eat anything today that I saw."

She didn't hear him, lost in her search. He shook his head, then went on a search for food for her. Returning to the office, he saw she was on her feet, pacing, eyes staring at her bookshelves.

"It was here, Doug. I know it was. So, where did it go?"

"The yearbooks? I don't know, Darcy. Is it okay if I look through your cupboards in here? And you're sure you unpacked everything?"

She nodded. "I always unpack everything. I don't like boxes sitting around." She stopped. "Wait, check the utility room. There may be some boxes in there, though I don't think so."

Doug was back, yearbooks in hand. "Found them. They were stuck in the back of a cupboard in there."

"Now why would I put them there? That's not like me."

"No, it's not, Darcy. Have you had any problems with your security system?"

She shook her head. "None. I change my password every week, and the keypad is not where it can be seen through a window."

She turned back to his yearbooks, then reached for hers. "There's something different about yours than mine."

"Bring them with you. I've got some soup and sandwiches ready. You need to eat."

She leafed through the two sets of books, studying page by page. Finally, her hand froze as she turned the pages, and a chill ran down her.

"There, Doug. Do you see? Yours IS different from mine."

"Where?" As she pointed out the difference, he nodded. "You're right and this could well be the clue we need. I need to take both books with me and give them to Caleb. He'll get them to the task force for us."

She nodded. "I just pray this is what we need. We still have to find them though."

Doug looked over at her, then reached for her hand. "We will, Darcy, we will. Now, I'm out of here. Lock up after me and get some rest."

"You need that too, Doug. You can't continue as you are."

He shrugged. "I'm used to it, being on call. Which reminds me, I'm on call again for the next twenty-four hours. If you need me, call me."

She just shook her head as she locked up. Then her eyes raised to the ceiling, she prayed. When will it end, Lord? And I really don't see a purpose here in all this, but I guess You do.

Doug tracked Caleb down the next morning, handing over the books and letting him know what Darcy had discovered. Caleb promised to pass them on to the task force, at the same time wondering what she would come up with next from that bottomless pit she called a memory.

Tom Allison sank down onto the bench outside the building. It had been a brutal twenty-four hour shift. Two calls that had lasted hours, only to end in peaceful resolution. Thank you for the negotiators, Lord, but we could do with a bit less tension right now.

Doug dropped down beside him. "How are the men?"

Tom shook his head. "This is taking a lot out of them. I don't know how much longer we can go on, and the other two shifts are the same."

Doug nodded. "I hear you. We had a meeting with the task force leaders yesterday and are working through some new information. Hopefully this will lead us to the suspect."

Tom leaned his head back and closed his eyes against the rising sun. "I hope it does."

"Don't fall asleep out here, Tom. Head on home."

Chapter 16

Darcy raised her head from her paperwork in the back of the shop as she heard voices, then steps heading her way. She paused, reaching for the weapon she had in her desk drawer, then withdrew her hand when she saw who it was.

"You look awful, Doug. You shouldn't be here."

He smiled. "And good morning to you, too. Up for a coffee break?"

She shook her head. "No, I'm not. I need to get through this paperwork to get intfiled."

"What can I do to help?"

"Really? Then go get some sleep. You're sleep walking, you know."

He leaned against the counter she was working on and studied her face. "Did you get any sleep yourself?"

"I did, more than I have in a while." She leaned back. "Now, will you get out of here and go get some sleep."

"Only if you let me come take you to dinner."

"A bargain, I see. Can I let you know tomorrow?"

Mirth sparkled in his eyes as he shook his head. "Still haven't forgotten that line, I see. I'll be back about closing time. I'm glad Abby's here with you. By the way, did you offer her a permanent position?"

"I'm thinking of it. Why?"

"I heard today she's tendered her resignation. I guess she really did mean what she said about finding a new career path."

"Thanks for the heads up. I'll talk with her. She has taken to this so well." She looked up at him. "Now, will you get out of here?"

He hesitated, then leaned forward to drop a kiss on her cheek before turning and walking away. Darcy's hand went to her cheek as she stared after him. No, she thought, he really didn't, did he? It was a while before she turned back to her paperwork, lost in thoughts of what could have been and what might still be.

"Abby, do you have a moment?" Darcy went to find her mid-morning.

"I do. What's wrong?"

"Absolutely nothing. I hear by the grapevine you're resigning from the force."

"Doug. I might have known."

"Hey, be careful there. He just let me know so I could offer you a full-time permanent position if you want it."

Abby's eyes grew round with surprise and she couldn't speak. Finally, getting words out, she asked, "Do you really mean it?"

Darcy nodded. "I do. This shop has taken off so well, I can't do both it and the online store. If you want to take over the shop, then I can concentrate on the online store and finding us our treasures."

"Darcy, this is wonderful. So where do we go from here?"

"Well, we could close up and go for lunch, or we could order in and start our planning."

"Order in. This is just great."

Bill Watson walked into Caleb's office that afternoon. "What new material has she provided?"

"That lady has a mind like a steel trap. I don't think she ever forgets anything. Doug said after they got back last night, she went looking through their yearbooks, and found a discrepancy between hers and his. I've marked the pages."

Bill studied the two pages. "How does this happen? They're both printed from the same run, likely."

Caleb nodded. "After all this time, we'll not likely find out why, but I have an officer following up on that. Any word on the person behind it all?"

"Not yet, but we've gotten some strong leads. It's a matter of working through them. How's Darcy doing with all this?"

"Doug says okay. He's the one that was exhausted. He was on call for the last day or so. He said Darcy told him to go away and get some sleep. He's planning on taking her out."

"What is going on with those two, anyway?"

"You don't know their history? They were dating in college, just about engaged. Then Doug walked away, knowing he was choosing law enforcement for a career, and didn't think it fair to a wife to be waiting at home for bad news."

Bill shook his head. "They don't learn, do they? Having the right partner makes it that much easier."

Caleb agreed, then looked up as Eddie appeared in his doorway. "What do you have, Eddie?"

"Hi, Bill. We've tracked down the printer for that yearbook. They were asked to do a couple of books, like the one Darcy had, separate from the rest of the run, and paid well for it. The name that was given doesn't exist, but there was a credit card used. We trying to track that down now, but there's not a lot of hope we'll find out anything."

"We'll pray you do, Eddie." Bill stood. "I need to head back. Let me know what you find out."

Eddie watched Bill walk away, then turned back to Caleb.

"Shut the door, Eddie."

Eddie did so, then sank into one of the chairs, grateful for a chance to be off his feet. "What's on your mind, Caleb?"

"This whole thing. I know Darcy's right, there's someone behind it all, but I don't think it's coming from the college. Can you run with this and see if you can find out if any law enforcement people were involved in that group? We'd be looking at someone late 40s to their 60s, even retired by now."

"I don't like that thought, Caleb, but I see what you're getting at. What has happened—there has had to be someone with more knowledge than what you get off the internet."

Caleb nodded. "And I hate to suspect a fellow officer, but that's the way it's heading. Doug mentioned that he had a call from an old professor. Find out who that was and follow that up."

"This is just getting stranger and stranger and bigger and bigger. It's like a hurricane building."

"I know, Eddie, and I feel like we're in the eye, just waiting for the other wall to move in. We haven't had any incidents in a couple of days. We're due for one."

Eddie nodded as he stood. "That we are. Let's pray we find this guy before he hits again." Eddie's eyes strayed to the door. "How well do you know Bill Watson?"

"Not as well as I know some others, just since I became chief. Why?"

"He fits the age group you're looking at." Eddie turned back to find Caleb watching him, a closed look on his face. "I would hate it to be him."

"You and me both. While you're at it, check out all the task force leaders. Better yet, get in touch with Tracker's. They have better resources than we do, it seems. Have them run the names we're looking at."

"I'll personally see to that, keeping it between you and me. Doing the search off site is wise." Eddie hesitated, then walked away.

Caleb sat back, horror running through him. If it was Bill Watson, then he knew everything he did. He would have to be very careful from now on. Lord, we need your help right now. Eddie's raised a possibility I had never thought of. Protect us, protect Darcy.

Chapter 17

Doug was waiting when Darcy closed up that night. She turned to find him beside her.

"Doug, weren't you just here?"

"I was and now I'm back. Dinner?"

"Just like that. You show up and say "dinner"? I'm not a dog you know."

"Maybe you should get one."

She shook her head. "Not happening. I don't have time for that."

"Then how am I supposed to ask you out for a walk, if I can't use your dog as an excuse?"

She stopped, eyes narrowing at the mischief in his face. "Doug. You have to stop."

"No, I don't and no, I won't. Would you please have dinner with me?"

"People will talk, you know. They already are."

He shrugged. "So, let them. Come on. We can go to Mac's or somewhere else."

She huffed. "Mac's it is. I need to put my briefcase back inside."

"Here, I'll drop it into my truck."

Ian watched as Doug and Darcy seated themselves at Doug's favourite booth in the back. "That's interesting."

"What is?" Murphy's eyes rose from the menu he was studying.

"Doug and Darcy. They both tried to tell Abe nothing was going on."

"Darcy? That's her?"

Ian turned to Murphy. "I forgot. You didn't get to meet her the other day. Just be careful. Abe was telling stories about your ladies, and now she wants to meet each one. She figures she can refine their runaway plans."

Murphy shook his head, then stopped. "Can you feel it, Ian?"

Ian nodded. "He's here somewhere. I wish I knew what he looked like."

"They don't have pictures?"

"Abe didn't say if they did or not."

Darcy scanned the menu and set it back. "I don't know why I look at that. Mac will just bring me what he thinks I should have."

"He will or if you insist, I'll go head him off and let you choose."

She shook her head. "No, it's fine whatever he brings." She looked at Doug, seeing the fine lines in his face that never used to be there, and the faint dusting of gray at his temples. "Have you heard anything?"

He shook his head. "No, but I know Caleb's running some separate investigations he's not talking about."

They were headed for Doug's truck when a voice stopped them, Ian and Murphy walking towards them.

Upon learning Murphy's name, Darcy pointed at him. "Adriel's Murphy. I need to meet your lady."

Murphy stared at her, not helped by the laughter erupting from Doug and Ian. "You do?"

"I do. I need to know how she planned her run."

Murphy shook his head. "Sorry, I can't do that."

"Of course, you can."

"No, I really mean that. She's out of town right now."

"Well, when's she back, I want to meet her and Matt's Sarah. And Abe's sister and sister-in-law."

Ian stared at her. "How do you do that? Abe only mentioned their names and connections once that I can remember."

Doug answered for her. "She's always been able to remember names and connections. A good thing or a bad thing, depending on the circumstances."

Doug's phone rang at that point, and he stepped away to take the call. Ian, facing him, saw the grim lines that settled on his face and knew that there had been another incident.

"Darcy, we need to go. Catch up with you two later."

Murphy watched them walk away. "What's that all about, Ian?"

"Something else has happened, I would suspect."

Darcy settled into her seat, then turned to Doug. "Where was it and how?"

"How do you know it was another one?"

"Your face. You don't hide it well."

He sighed. "You're right. He hit a fire station tonight. They have two men in hospital."

"This guy is really getting to me," she stated. "We need to stop this. The casualty count is too high."

"We're heading for Caleb's, if that's all right. He wants to talk to you, but away from the office."

She froze. "Is this about the yearbooks?"

Doug shrugged. "He didn't say. He'll be there is about ten minutes. Hannah and the boys are out, so we'll be on our own."

"I still don't like it, Doug. It's hitting too close to home now."

Caleb settled into his chair in the living room and faced the two sitting on the couch near him. He was glad that Hannah and their two boys were out for the night.

"Talk to us, Caleb. Tell us what's happening."

"As I said in the text, he hit again this morning. The two firefighters have been discharged from the hospital. This guy has no regard for any life at all." Caleb watched Darcy's face. "We've taken a look at your yearbooks. Darcy, yours was one of only two in a special run, paid for to be different."

She stared at him. "A different run. How is that even possible?"

"Eddie tracked it down. The company was paid well for those two books. We're trying to run who paid as the name given was false. We also tracking down if any law enforcement people were as part that group."

"Law enforcement—as in already on a force?" Doug's quiet question broke the silence that had followed Caleb's words.

Caleb nodded. "That's what we're looking at right now. The guy has too much knowledge of how emergency forces operate to be doing this by chance. This means someone in law enforcement is pushing from behind the scenes."

Darcy sat back, close enough to Doug that her shoulder brushed his. She was lost in thought and didn't feel his arm come around her or his eyes on her. Caleb watched and nodded. Hannah, you are right again. Their feelings never died.

"So, what you are saying is that I received a "special" yearbook, we have someone running the show, and I am still a target as is anyone in that group. Correct?" Her eyes found Caleb's. At his nod, she continued, "Have you tracked down all the members of that group?"

"Most of them, I think Frankie said. He's been working on that with some of the task force. And before you ask, everyone we talked to has been connected in some way to the incidents. So, your suspicion is correct."

"I wish it wasn't, Caleb." She stood and paced. "So where do we stand now?"

"Have you had any more thoughts on who it might be?"

She nodded and then sighed, sitting back down by Doug, his arm drawing her close once again. "Get out your pen and paper." She began listing names.

Caleb and Doug exchanged more than one glance at the names. "How are you coming up with these, Darcy? I need to know how in order to explain that to the task force."

"I don't want you to give these to the task force yet, as I am not certain how they would fit it. Do you have someone who can trace them for you?"

Caleb nodded. "He's working on a list of names for me now. Let me call him."

"Tracker's, Jace."

"Jace, it's Caleb Logan."

"Caleb, I was going to call you in a bit. I have some information for you."

"Can I put you on speaker then, Jace? I have Doug Foster, our ETF lieutenant, and Darcy O'Shaughnessy with me."

"Darcy. Sure, go ahead."

Caleb set his phone on the coffee table so they all could hear. "We're set, Jace."

"Darcy, my girl, how are you?"

Her face alight, she recognized the voice of an old friend. "Jace. How are you? And Emma?"

"We're fine now. Good to hear your voice again. You're living here now?"

"I am. We'll need to get together."

"We will, at some point. But first. Caleb, are you sure you want them to hear?"

"Unless it's that bad, yes. Let me ask. The top name—initials WW."

Jace sighed. "How'd you know that?"

"Just a guess. Let's set that one aside for now and you can send me that information by courier."

"No, I'll meet you at Mac's 6 a.m. tomorrow. Now, your other names."

Jace ran through all the names he had been given. There were a couple who were red flagged and he was doing more research. "Other than that one name, they're clear. But you have more names, I can tell."

"I do. Darcy, give him the names."

"Jace, these are the names," and she proceeded to give them to him. "This is that group we were part of. Come to think of it, Emma was in it for a couple of months before she quit."

"She mentioned that last night when I said your name. She never had a good feeling about it and that's why she left. She was surprised you stayed."

"I didn't want to. Something made me though, even with the uncomfortable feelings and vibes I got from two or three of the people. You often mentioned the very same names."

They could hear quiet over the phone, then Jace spoke, "The very same ones?"

Darcy nodded, then realized she needed to speak. "The very same. Now as to faculty and staff, these are the ones who were involved. Outside involvement would be these ones."

Caleb and Doug exchanged glances at the names she was giving. How did she do it, Caleb wondered once again.

"Okay. Caleb, I'll run with these. I'll see you at Mac's at 6."

Caleb sat back, thoughts swirling through his head. Bill Watson. If he was truly involved, then how did they investigate? He would need to be very careful.

He looked up to find the others' eyes on him.

"Bill Watson. Right, Caleb?" Darcy's voice was soft and full of pain. "I trusted him. Now, I can't."

Caleb sighed. "Yes, that's who he was talking about. I don't like it either, Darcy. I'll see what Jace has for me tomorrow. So, you know Jace?"

"I do, from college and then from after. I've worked with him on a number of cases. Emma, too." She turned to Doug. "Do you remember Jace?"

"The nerd?"

She swatted him. "The nerd as you jocks called him. He was more into sports than you realized. Elle and I used to go running with him and Emma. We used to run for hours, planning on all of us entering a marathon at some point."

Caleb stopped his mug halfway to his mouth. "Elle?"

She nodded. "Adriel was her full name, but we called her Elle."

Doug's eyes met Caleb's, then the both smiled. "I'm glad to tell you she's living here in town. Murphy, one of Abe's men, is dating her."

"And now you're going to tell me she's one of those he tried to protect and she ran too. I need to talk to these ladies to find out their secrets."

Caleb's eyes sought Doug as Doug erupted in laughter. "You weren't with us the other day. Abe was telling her how all the ladies would run in this town, especially the ones they were to protect. Frankie had already told her about Deirdre. Darcy has decided she needs to meet them all so that she can learn their techniques and refine them."

Caleb shook his finger at her. "No, that's not happening. We have enough trouble. We don't need you running added to that."

She shook her head. "Here, I thought that would be the ideal solution. Guess not, huh?"

"No." Doug pulled her to her feet and led her to the door. "Keep us updated, Caleb."

"Come see me in the morning, Doug. You're on call?"

Doug nodded. "In the morning, then."

He watched as Doug and Darcy left Caleb's and headed back to Darcy's. His vehicle left the curb and he followed cautiously. Why had they been meeting him? Had he been found out? The voices

were getting louder and louder. He wouldn't
soon be able to tell one from the other.

Chapter 18

Doug closed the door to Caleb's office and sat, waiting until Caleb was free of the paperwork he was working on. Finally, he sat back and looked at Doug.

"Where's Darcy?"

"At her shop. You do realize you lost an officer?"

Caleb nodded. "I know. That's part of the reason I approached her. She had talked to me of leaving. Fitting in all right, is she?"

"Well enough that Darcy has asked her to run the physical shop while she concentrates on the online one. What's up, Caleb?"

"You guessed it was Bill Watson Jace dug up the information on."

Doug nodded. "I gathered that. What did he find?"

"Not what I wanted to hear." He handed over the pages Jace had given him that morning.

"Wow! This is not good," Doug commented as he read. "And he knows we have Darcy with us." He looked up at Caleb. "You know he's going to hit us last, and it will be a big one."

Caleb nodded. "That's my fear, and there is no way we can prepare for it totally. For now, I'm assigned patrol to any EMS call. Officers are willing to work as much overtime as I will allow. Your squad and the other two will be on call all the time. It's a lot to put on your guys."

"It is what it is. Hopefully it will be over soon." Doug stopped, his thumb running around the rim of the cup he had picked up. "You know, Darcy's getting ready to go to the media, to make herself a target."

"I know. We have to prevent that. I'll even help her run if it comes to that. You'll go with her."

Doug looked up in surprise, sure Caleb was joking, but he caught the serious look in his eyes, and nodded. "I'm sure you will. It's coming to that. At least with Abby in the shop, she won't worry as much. My concern is when she goes out looking for her treasures as she calls them. She goes on her own.”

Caleb sat back. “I can’t bring in anyone else. Abe’s volunteered his men, but they’re busy enough unless it comes to a crisis.” He looked at Doug, studying him. “How’s the head?”

Doug looked up. “It’s fine. I have clearance to be back to all my duties.” He looked at Caleb and shook his head. “No, Caleb, not that card. I won’t do it to my men.”

“I know you won’t and I won’t even suggest it. It’s just that I know concussions can be tricky, even mild ones.” Caleb looked down at the paperwork Doug had returned to him. “Now I have to decide how to deal with Bill Watson.”

“Be yourself, Caleb. Don’t let on what you know. If you can, keep your contact to the phone or text or email. He’ll read you. You hide your emotions well after all these years, but this is something neither one of us have faced before. You’re not on the task force, which helps.”

"I wasn't but I was asked to step in for someone who became ill. I hadn't responded yet."

"Send someone else. Eddie would be good to send."

"He would be, wouldn't he? He can read people well. This is when I wish Ben Johnson hadn't retired."

"Ben excelled at his job. Can we get him back as a consultant, at least?"

Caleb shook his head. "He's deep into business with Abe, teaching at his training facility. He would come if we asked, but I would rather not."

Doug stood, hesitating as he moved to the door. "Sometimes, Caleb, I wish I had chosen a different line of work. But then, God led me this way, and I know I have to trust. It's hard, especially when I realize what I did to Darcy all those years ago."

"Don't beat yourself up, Doug. That was in God's hands too. If you two had married, Darcy wouldn't have the knowledge today that we need. She wouldn't have walked the path God needed her to walk."

Doug stood, staring at the door, digesting the words Caleb had said. Caleb watched his friend, compassion in his eyes. Doug finally nodded and walked out the door, closing it quietly behind him.

Doug's thoughts were on what Caleb had told him. How did they keep what they had learned from him? He prayed as he walked back to his office and sat, contemplating his paperwork.

Tom knocked at his door and then entered, closing the door. "What's the word, Doug? I'm hearing rumours."

Doug sat back, already tired. "It's not good, Tom. We've just been put to being on call twenty-four/seven as have the other two teams. Caleb's sending patrols out with every EMS call. We're in a war, my friend, and we aim to win."

Tom shook his head. "This is really going to wear on the men."

"I know. What we'll do is still have one team on site, the other two can be off site but have their pagers handy at all times, going about their business as much as they can. Have the team leaders monitor the men and get back to me if they need someone off for any time, even a day. We'll cover for each other. That's what we do."

Tom nodded. "Now about Darcy. What's happening with her?"

"She just keeps getting in deeper and deeper. We've traced it back to a group both of us was in during college. Every incident has been aimed at someone in that group."

Tom sat back, stunned at what Doug had just told him. "Every one?" At Doug's nod, he absorbed what he was saying. "That's makes it hard to figure out who."

"Darcy's already done that, and also figured out that he's not acting on his own. There's someone behind him, and she's thinking law enforcement."

Tom stared at him. "That makes bizarre sense, you know. I couldn't figure out how one man, and a civilian at that, would have the knowledge of our movements to know when and how to hit."

"Keep that under your hat. We don't want word getting out at all."

Tom nodded. "Make sure you take time for yourself too, Doug. I hear you've been seen around town with our newest shop owner."

Doug smiled, shaking his head. "Go to work, Tom. We're just old friends."

"That's not what I'm hearing."

"For now, that's all it is."

Tom laughed as he left, pulling out his phone to make the calls he needed to.

Doug shook his head again. Was it that obvious to everyone? No wonder Darcy was making the comments she was. They weren't as quiet about their relationship as they thought. He stood, a thought running through his mind. His feet led him to Mac's.

Finding Mac in his office, he shut the door and sat. "Mac, what's the rumbling you're hearing on the street?"

Mac grinned. "About you and Darcy? That you make a really cute couple and why haven't you had her around before." He studied his nephew, seeing the new lines in his face. "But that's not why you're here."

"No. But tell everyone I'm working on it, okay? Trying to court her in all this craziness is hard." Doug paused, gathering his thoughts. "What are you hearing about what's going on with the attacks?"

Mac sat back. "I wondered when you would come and find me about that. I'm hearing police involvement. Not this town." Mac stopped, watching his nephew. "It's not what you want to hear, I can tell."

"We've already come to that conclusion, Mac. Who, do you have a name?"

Mac nodded. "You'll need to watch your lady, Doug. Word out is that he's after her as well."

Doug paled. "It must be someone pretty high up for you to be saying that."

Mac nodded. "It is. Is this the name?" When he said it, Doug's eyes slid shut. Mac had just confirmed their worst fears.

"It is, Mac. Now we have to figure out how to catch him, without him catching us first."

"God will lead, Doug. I have a feeling your troubles are just starting in this town, that it will get worse and worse. To that end, SuEllen has set up a prayer chain that works all day and all night, until this is over. The response was overwhelming. We have you covered in prayer every minute of every hour of every day. Take care of your lady, Doug. That's what I would ask of you."

"It's going to be hard, Mac. Caleb's just put us on call twenty-four/seven for the next while."

"You'll get there. Spend time with her. I hope you're taking my suggestions."

"I am. Darcy asked me what I was up to and I informed her I was told to court her. She looked surprised at that."

"She's a special lady, Doug. She deserves that. If you two had married years ago, you wouldn't be ready to face what you are now."

Doug stared at him. "You're the second person to say that to me today."

"God speaks when and where we least expect him. Heed his words, Doug, and lean on Him in these perilous times. Be a David,

Doug. Go back to the Psalms and study how David reacted to being pursued and persecuted."

Doug nodded as he stood. "Thanks, Mac. I appreciate your words and advice."

He watched as Doug walked away from the cafe. What had he been up to? It wasn't a mealtime, so why was he there? Eyes turning to the cafe, then back to Doug, he followed Doug, shrugging. Maybe something, maybe nothing. He needed to finish his plans for Riverville. He was told he would need to start soon.

Chapter 19

Doug stood watching as Darcy finished for the day, eyes scanning the area. He could feel something in the air around them, not a good feeling that he knew. He had heard others speaking of feeling evil. He had scoffed, but not anymore.

Darcy came towards him, a smile on her face, one he remembered from days past. One she reserved just for him. Did she realize that she wore that smile again? He reached for her hand and pulled her along the street with him.

"Doug, slow down. My feet are tired and I can't run in these shoes."

"Sorry." He slowed his steps. "I forgot for a minute we weren't back in college and you weren't wearing the sneakers you liked to wear."

"I did, didn't I? So where are we off to?"

"Here." He had stopped in front of a shop.

"Flowers, Doug?"

He nodded. "I want to do this courting thing right, and flowers are part of it. Even though you deserve every flower I could ever give you." He opened the door and ushered her in.

"What kind of flowers are you looking for, Doug, for your lovely lady?" Anna, the florist, had a huge smile on her face. She felt she had read the signs right.

Darcy glared at Doug, then turned to smile at Anna. "Show me your daisies, Anna. They're my favourite flowers."

"This way. Close your mouth, Doug, you'll catch flies." She laughed at the expression on Doug's face.

"Daisies, Darcy?"

She nodded. "You used to bring me daisies when you had a few dollars to spend on flowers. They were cheap, I know, but it meant so much that you would bring any kind of flower to me."

"Daisies, it is, Anna, then."

Darcy laid her flowers on her knee, then turned to Doug as he started his truck.

"What's going on, Doug? I know you well enough to know something is."

He sighed, then turned to her, eyes serious, the mischief usually there missing. "There is, and I just don't know how to tell you. Let me drive you to somewhere we can walk and talk. SuEllen packed us a picnic supper if you want to eat."

"That would be nice. Does your river have a picnic area? I haven't had a chance to explore that area much."

"It does."

Doug stuffed their supper garbage back into the bag, then walked over to dump it in the trash can, trying to sort out his thoughts. I could use some help here, Lord.

Darcy watched the conflicting emotions cross the face she loved. She had finally admitted it. She had never stopped loving him.

As Doug seated himself across from her once more, she reached for his hands. "Start where you're always told to start. At the beginning."

Doug's eyes strayed beyond her, looking at the peaceful scene created by the flowing water of the river, the bending of the willow trees over it, the reeds in the shallow water. He listened to the calls of the birds, the insects, and the frogs. He brought his eyes back to Darcy's eyes, seeing her feelings in them that she hadn't been ready for him to see before.

"This is hard, Darcy. So very hard. It's not what we ever expected when we began this investigation into law enforcement." He stopped, gathering his thoughts, unable to continue for a few minutes. "Eddie's done some digging, as has Frankie. Jace came through in a way that we never expected. He narrowed our search to one man."

"Bill Watson." Her voice was low, barely audible.

Doug nodded. "I don't know how you knew, but that's who we're looking at."

She sighed as his hands tightened on hers. "I think I always knew. There was just something about him. I never felt comfortable around him." She thought about him. "You don't remember him, do you?"

Doug shook his head. "Was he part of the group?"

She thought about that. "Not really. He wanted to be but not one of us would accept him. We turned to others for our research and advice. He never said anything, but one day when he had been rebuffed, I saw the pure rage and hatred in his eyes. Come to think of it, he was close with that student whom we had problems with."

Doug shook his head. "I don't remember that at all."

"Come to think of it, you weren't there that day. Jace was but I don't know if he remembers it. It happened so fast and in a quiet way."

"I'll check with him later. Right now, we have to make plans on how to keep you safe from him. Chances are he's already figured out you've remembered him."

"Oh, I'm sure he has. Now, can we put that aside for now? This is too pretty an area to talk about life and death."

"That we can do. Like to go for a walk?"

She shook her head. "Not tonight. Let's find a bench where we can watch the water."

Seated on a bench facing the river, his arm drew her close to his side. They just sat, digesting what had gone on around them in the last few weeks.

"How many people know of your suspicions?"

"Caleb, Eddie, Frankie, Jace, you, me. We've kept it really quiet. Caleb went to Tracker's to keep it out of the department itself."

"That's good. Now you have to gather evidence, and that will be tough, given he knows procedures and how to hide."

"We'll find it, somehow, and it will be legal and stand in court."

She nodded, then turned to look at him. "And us, Doug, where do we stand?"

"I know where I'd like us to stand, but we need to get through this trial first. Both Caleb and Mac had an interesting observation today, almost word for word the same.”

“And that would be?”

Doug wrapped her tighter in his arms and dropped his head to hers. “Both said we weren’t meant to marry after college. That we both needed to go through what we have to be prepared for today. That you wouldn’t have the experience or the knowledge to help if we had married.”

She stilled and thought about that. Was it true, Lord? Did You plan this all these years ago and I wasted time resenting You for that? She sighed. “I guess I wasted a few years being mad at God, then.”

“Were you mad at Him?”

“At Him and at you. I never ever expected to run into you at Mac’s that day or to be sitting here with you. God has a plan, Doug.”

“He does. Are you prepared to walk all the way through?”

“I have to be. I can’t walk away from all those people, even if it means my death. God knows the path we walk. I am just beginning to realize just how much He leads."

"And you're okay with that?" Doug hated to think of losing her, but the reality was there that neither one of them might survive.

"I am. Are you?"

"I have to be. I have to accept that reality every time I go on a call. Nothing is guaranteed, not in this life."

She shivered, suddenly feeling an evil around them. "Let's go, Doug. He's here somewhere."

Doug rose, drawing her up with him and tucking her into his truck, eyes searching the growing twilight.

"Do you have a weapon?"

She nodded. "I have the proper license as well as I worked with the police and kept up any credentials I thought I'd need. I carry it from now on. Abby has hers as well."

Caleb tracked Doug down the next day. "We've got a hit on our suspect. We now have confirmation of his name. We're working on an address for him."

"Somehow, I don't think he'll be alive when we get there." Doug was not optimistic they would find him in time.

"I'm not either. I've put Team B on alert to go with us. I want you to stay out of the takedown."

Doug nodded. "That's fine with me. Any more incidents?"

"Not that I've heard about. But it's only a matter of time."

Doug shuddered at the thought. "I know, and it's going to be us. Somehow, I think he'll go after all of us at once."

Caleb studied Doug's face. "Why do you say that?"

"His last stand will be here. He'll want to make it a big one, take out as many as he can. He won't care if civilians are caught in the crossfire."

"And we can't clear out the town. Life goes on, no matter what we think will happen. How'd Darcy take the news?"

"She wasn't surprised at all. She remembers his being there at some of the meetings and befriending our suspect." He shook his head. "Her memory is scary."

"It will be more than scary if word gets out she remembers."

"I let her know only select people knew who we suspected. She's fine with that." He stopped, unable to continue.

"Doug?" Caleb's voice held concern. "What did she say?"

"She said she was fine with everything, even if it meant her death. She also told me she wasted time being mad at God and she wasn't mad at him anymore. Mac basically told me what you did the other day. When I mentioned it to Darcy, she was in total agreement." Doug looked up at his chief and friend. "So how do reconcile our fears and dreams, Caleb? How do we get through this?"

"Lots of prayer, Doug, and we have that. That's what will get us through, prayer and our faith. If you need to talk, come find me."

Caleb moved away, pulling out his phone as it dinged. Bill Watson, he wanted to meet and talk. Not yet, Bill. We'll do it by phone.

Caleb set his phone down later in the day and stared at it. That was the strangest conversation he had ever had with another law enforcement person. Bill was fishing, and not in a very subtle way. Caleb shook his head. He could feel the situation escalating. Instead of feeling like he was in the centre of a hurricane, today he felt like he was standing on the top of a volcano ready to erupt and send destroying lava flowing in all directions.

Eddie chose that moment to knock at his door, enter and close it behind him. Sinking into a chair, he studied Caleb.

"Regretting taking on the role of chief?"

Caleb nodded. "Some days are like that. I just got off the phone with Bill

Watson. He's probing for information and not very subtly either."

"We're getting more information on him. Jace is good. Whoever trained him, they did it well."

"What do you have?"

Eddie handed over the paperwork he had been holding. "That's the only copy in the office. Jace keeps the original and met up with me to deliver that. He suggested we destroy it after you had seen it."

Caleb read through it, his heart sinking even further. "How did he get away with this for so long?"

"He knows how to hide the evidence. I have a feeling we're not going to find our suspect alive, if we even find him." He turned to look at the door. "There's a lot of rumbling in the ranks. They're frustrated and while not turning on one another, they're sniping, and that's not our crew."

Caleb nodded. "I know. Let me talk with them, one shift at a time. Set it up. Have Mac cater for us, lunch type stuff that will keep. Do what you have to do to keep their spirits up."

"I know God's in control, Caleb, but it would be nice if once in a while, He shared His plans with us. It would make it easier." On that note, Eddie walked away, leaving Caleb staring after him.

That's so not like Eddie, Lord. Bring him comfort and peace. Lead us how you would have us go.

Doug stood in the doorway, watching his friend's bent head.

"Caleb."

Caleb looked up and waved him in. "What's up, Doug?"

"I have that paperwork you wanted for the shifts. I've talked to all the team leaders and they're on board with our plans. We just need to figure out what to do with them once this is over. We'll need to compensate in some way."

"We'll figure it out. Money won't be the answer." Caleb's phone rang at that point, and he looked with puzzlement at the number. "Don't go, Doug. I need to take this call, but we need to speak further on this."

Caleb shut off his phone, deep in thought. Then his eyes strayed to Doug, watching the expressions crossing Caleb's face.

"Good news or bad news?"

Caleb thought. "Good news for once. That was the president of one of our big manufacturers. He's got together with others in town, and they have an offer for us when this is all over. They plan to send families away for a week's vacation on one of their private islands."

Doug was surprised, then wondered why he would be. "God is planning ahead, isn't He?"

"He is, Doug. We forget that He's planning for our good, not our bad. In the depraved world we live in it's had to keep track of that. Now, your paperwork. Let's see it and I'll sign off on it. Make sure all of the teams are able to get down time when they're not on site. I trust you've worked that out. By the way, Eddie mentioned there's rumblings. I'll be talking to each shift, a shift at a time. I've asked him to arrange with Mac to cater for us."

"Mac's been expecting that, Caleb. He's already made plans. Don't expect to pay him though. He's doing it for you and he's been getting donations without even asking. The town is behind all of us."

Caleb sat back. "Now, that's refreshing to hear. Make sure you pass on to the others the town's behind us. It will help to bolster morale."

Doug was waiting for Darcy once again as she turned from the counter. She waved at Abby as she left, Doug reaching for her hand. It had become a habit for them to eat together after a day's work, if they were able to.

Seated at Mac's, Darcy looked around. "How long has it been since we've been under siege, Doug?"

He shrugged. "I'm not sure, but at least six weeks. Why?"

"So, it's only been six weeks since we reconnected? It feels at times that we never had that multi-year break."

"It does, doesn't it?" Doug watched her face intently, wondering where she was going with this.

"So, you really think God had planned all this? To bring us together, separate us, and then bring us together? Or did we cause a wrinkle in His plans by separating from each other?"

"I don't think we'll ever know here on earth, Darcy. Why do you ask?"

She shrugged. "Just asking, I guess. I'm still trying to work it all out."

After their meal, Doug checked out what shoes she was wearing. Good, he thought, we can walk tonight. "Walk with me, Darcy?"

She nodded, hand held in his strong grasp. She had missed that, his strength and caring coming through that contact.

Talk moved through a various number of topics until Doug stopped on a bridge that ran over a stream in the park in the centre of town. He stared down at the water, searching for words.

Darcy stood beside him, close enough he could feel the fabric of her blouse against his bare arm. He then turned and led her past there to a bench overlooking the river.

Pulling her down, he wrapped her in his arms.

"Darcy, so much is going on, we haven't had time to talk about us? Is there an us?"

She nodded. "I would like to think there would be, Doug, when this is all over."

"Why do we wait until it's all over? Can't we have an "us" now?"

She turned her head to look at him. "Now?"

He nodded. "We're not guaranteed tomorrow, Darcy. I would hate to lose you without you knowing that you're the only one I will ever love or spend my life with." He looked down into her tear-filled eyes. "I'm sorry. I made you cry. Forget what I said."

She shook her head. "No, Doug. You've said what you've needed to say for years. I accept. You're the only one for me."

He watched her closely, then bent to kiss her. He drew back and watched her face. "I think we need to plan more of these."

She smacked him. "This type of planning doesn't work. So where do we go from here?"

"Where? First, I want to court you, as Mac has said. We don't know what tomorrow is going to bring for us, but will you accept the ring from me? It's the one I bought when we were in college. If you don't like it, we'll go find another one."

"No, Doug, the first ring is the one from your heart." Ring on her finger, she raised her face to him once again, then settled back into his arms.

"So, how do we plan for the future while trying to catch a killer?"

Doug started to laugh. "Only you, Darcy, could accept a marriage proposal, then plan to catch a killer. We're working on it. We're working on keeping you safe as well. Caleb's coming up with some plans."

"I hope his plans work better than Abe's did, or I'll have to find those ladies and get their ideas on how to run and refine them."

"Just promise me you'll take me with you, is all I ask. Besides, Caleb said he would help you run if it comes to that."

"Did he really? Of course, I couldn't run on my own. I would need you with me. Now, get me home and get yourself home. You tell me you're on call twentyfour/seven. You need to rest when you can."

He watched them rise from the bench and walk past him, without even noticing him. Soon, he thought, soon he would eliminate Doug and bring Darcy to her knees. She would pay. His hands went to his head. Those voices were just too loud now.

Chapter 21

Caleb moved through the department, stopping to speak with each officer. Morale was low, not knowing who was after them. Caleb sighed to himself and wondered how they would take it if it really was Bill Watson.

Seeing Eddie waiting for him, he walked towards him.

"Eddie, what do you have for me?"

Eddie looked around the large area with the desks, then nodded towards the front doors. "Let's walk, Caleb."

Once outside the men headed for the central park area. They seated themselves, Eddie hesitant to speak.

"What's on your mind, Eddie?"

Eddie sighed. "Peg and I had dinner with Ben and Marg Johnson last night. He was asking me about what's going on. I know you've retained him as a consultant even though he's retired. We talked. He let me know some information that I'm not too sure how to explain."

"Just say it."

"Ben said there had been rumours that Bill Watson had a son, about the age now of Doug and Darcy. He never acknowledged that he did. The scuttlebutt on the streets years ago was that the mother poisoned the son against all law enforcement personnel because of him. I'm working on tracking that down and have asked Jace to help. Word is also that the boy didn't have the intellectual skills to get ahead, but that at some point, he connected with Bill, without him knowing that was his father and that Bill got him on that force and up through the ranks. I just pray Ben's memories are wrong, but I doubt it."

Caleb sat back to absorb what Eddie had said. "That makes sense, you know. Perfect sense. Do we know where the son is and the name?"

"We're working on a name. Ben had a run-in with him years ago and was going to go back through his notebooks to find it. I have a feeling he's here in town and being used in the other towns."

Caleb stood. "I think you're right, Eddie. Now to find him before he does more damage."

Eddie stood as well as they headed back to the department. "I have another tidbit that I don't think you've heard. I talked to Dave Allison last night."

"And?" Caleb looked over at Eddie, then groaned. "Tell me they didn't."

Eddie nodded his head, smile in place. "Dave talked to Doug last night and had a hard time keeping Doug's feet on the ground. It's official now, Caleb. What they should have done years ago, they've gone and done now. They're engaged."

Caleb threw up his hands. "Of course they are. Why wouldn't they be? Do our dating couples in town, who are in danger, do anything else?"

"At least they didn't elope."

Caleb glared at him. "At least not yet."

"They won't. Doug's adamant on that, Dave said. They're working on what drove them apart and brought them back together.

They both realize they have to get through what's going on around them before they take the next step."

Caleb just shook his head. Lord, what next? Lead our steps and give us the wisdom and protection we need.

Frankie was waiting on the steps for them, a grim look on his face. Steps slowing, Caleb and Eddie approached.

"Where, Frankie?"

Frankie shook his head. "Not where, who. He's changed his strategy."

Caleb took the note Frankie offered him. "He wants Darcy and only Darcy. Why?"

Frankie shrugged. "Who knows? I would hate to think all this has been about him getting to her."

Eddie studied the note. "It's not, Frankie. It's about revenge and revenge in a big way. Darcy's just a part of it. He'll expand who he wants, I would suspect. Now we have to keep her safe. Doug will want to be with her all the time and he knows he can't."

Frankie looked up at the sky. "Did I hear the rumours right?"

"You did, Frankie. Now, let's get in so we can make some plans. Hopefully Ben comes through with a name for us." Caleb headed into the building, leaving Eddie and Frankie standing behind him.

"Ben?"

Eddie nodded. "Peg and I had dinner with them last night. Ben had some interesting information and is tracking down a name for us. Come on in and I'll let you know where we stand on that."

Bill Watson stood in his office, staring out the window. It was all coming apart, he thought. All those years of planning, and it was coming apart. He cursed, raised his hand to throw his cup, and then thought better of that. He needed to find that no-good boy. He refused to acknowledge him as his son. No son of his would be like that.

He turned to his desk and reached for his phone, then withdrew his hand. No, he had to play it safe and cool, he thought. Not yet could he reveal his hand.

Caleb turned as Doug walked towards him.

"Doug, you've something to tell me?"

Doug nodded, a small smile playing around his lips. "You could say that, Caleb. Can we talk?"

Caleb nodded. "Here or elsewhere?"

"Your office is fine." Doug waited until they were seated. "What's up with Bill Watson? Darcy said he's been trying to get in touch with her, and she's not returning his calls. She says she's had too many for her own peace of mind."

Caleb studied his friend's face, seeing the worry lines growing on his face. "We're looking at all the senior officers now, and he's one we're digging into his past. Why would Darcy be concerned?"

Doug shrugged. "I'm not sure if she's even got it straight in her mind yet why, but I can tell you, I didn't get good vibes from him lately."

Caleb sat back, wondering how much he should tell Doug. "Let me put it this way. If I had a suspicion about a law enforcement officer being involved, he would top my list. We have no concrete evidence as yet, though."

"Do we know if he was ever involved with our group at college?"

"No evidence yet, but we're exploring every avenue we can find. Eddie and Frankie are working that. But that's not all that's on your mind."

Doug shook his head. "It's not, Caleb. Darcy's sure she's being followed but she can't see anyone when she looks around. I've felt the same when I'm with her."

"I would suspect she would be. Keep as close an eye on her as you can, and if you can, make sure she's got someone with her. That's the best we can do for now."

Doug nodded. "It's frustrating, Caleb. He hasn't hit anywhere in a few days, and that anticipation is a killer." He stood to walk away, then turned back. "If it is who you think, how do we stop him?"

"I'm not sure that we can. He probably thinks he's invincible and we won't catch on. Or, what I think, is that he's already figured out we know and is trying to find out how much information we have. Have Darcy stall responding to him if at all possible. I'm pulling her off as of today."

"You may be pulling her off, but you know she'll still be working it."

"I know, and that scares me. Talk to your lady, get her to leave it alone."

Doug shook his head. "Won't happen. Once she sinks her teeth into something, she doesn't let go."

Chapter 22

Darcy stared at Abby as she spoke. "What do you mean, someone from out of town was looking for me? What did he look like?"

Abby leaned against the store counter. "Now, that's a puzzle. I would say he was wearing a disguise, but he seemed familiar, as if I knew him from somewhere. He seemed young, maybe around our ages or so, not much taller than you. I just don't know, Darcy. I know him from somewhere."

Darcy nodded. "You've seen so many people over the years on the force. That could be doing it to you."

Abby shook her head. "No, I don't think so. This is just recent that I saw him." Her eyes strayed across the store and to the outside. "Darcy, look. That's him, standing there by the pet store."

Darcy stared at the man. "You're right, he does look familiar. Here's my camera. Can you get a picture of him at all?"

"I can. You stay back from the window. It's obvious that he's watching for you."

"Just don't tell Doug."

"Don't tell Doug what?"

Darcy sighed. "What are you doing here? Aren't you on duty?"

Doug looked between the two women, then watched as Abby moved away to take her pictures. "I am, but that's not why I'm here. What's going on?"

"Promise me you won't go storming out of here to my defence?" Darcy stared at him until he finally nodded. "Abby said someone from out of town has been asking for me. Someone around our ages. Is it him, Doug?"

"Is that why Abby's pretending to take pictures of your stock, but is really taking pictures through the window?"

Abby nodded and spoke. "It is. The man who had asked about Darcy was outside but he's gone now, so you don't have to go charging out of here. Here's Darcy's camera. I got some pictures for you to track down this guy. We don't need him around here scaring away our customers."

Doug took the camera he was offered and scanned through the photos. He stopped at a close-up one. "Do you know who that is, Darcy?"

She looked at the picture. "That's that student we had to kick out of the group. What's he doing here? More importantly, how is he involved?"

"I don't know, Darcy, but I plan on finding out. Make sure you stay well away from him."

"Oh, I plan to. Now, go. Get those pictures to the task force and let them handle finding him in town."

Doug shook his head as he walked out of the store, then stood scanning the area. The man was gone, but he knew where Darcy worked, and more than likely, where she lived. How were they to keep her safe?

Eddie looked away from the photos Doug handed him. "He's here in town?"

Doug nodded. "Abby got these through the store window. He had been inside asking for her."

"We need to keep her out of there now. He's tracked her to there. Think she'll cooperate?"

Doug shrugged. "She might and she might not. It's a hard call to make."

"How busy is the online store? Busy enough she could work from home?"

Doug shook his head. "She needs to be at the store so she can pack and ship the items. That's a good thought but it won't work."

"Why is it nothing is ever easy anymore?" Eddie leant back again his desk. "So how do you want to do this?"

"Me?"

"Yeah, you. She's your lady, isn't she? How do we keep her safe?"

Doug shook his head at Eddie. "We can't lock her away anywhere, that won't work. We can't put security on her. She'll run more than likely and she's already threatened to find all the ladies who have run and find out their techniques so she can refine them."

"She's almost as scary as Deirdre."

"They would be close to a tie, I think. But seriously, Eddie, this guy's found her. I'm sure he's already passed on word that he has."

"I'm sure he has." Eddie paused as he pulled out his phone to look at the text message. "He has."

Doug reached slowly for the phone, eyes on Eddie. "A threat?"

Eddie nodded. "More than a threat, a direct warning."

Doug sank back into a chair as he read the message. "We have no way of tracking this."

Eddie shook his head. "We've tried. He's using pay-as-you-go phones with a phony name and address. We can't track him that way."

They both looked up as Frankie appeared in the doorway.

"We've had another incident, guys. This time, just outside town. Paramedics were called to a person down report and came under fire."

Doug was on his feet. "Everyone okay?"

"They are. They're taking the warnings to heart and being very cautious going into areas. They waited for police backup and whoever it was got restless and fired on them. They weren't close enough to have anything other than the ambulance dinged up a bit."

"That's getting too close to home, Frankie." Doug walked past him to go find his team.

Frankie watched him walk away, then turned to Eddie.

"Darcy's been found and someone was asking after her. Doug says Darcy's identified him as the one they kicked out of their college group. Now he's trying to figure out how to keep her safer than she is."

"Where do we stand with our other investigation?"

"Caleb's keeping it very quiet right now, but he's tracking the information we need to make the arrest. The thing is, will we have it in time?"

"It scares me that we won't, Frankie, and that we'll lose men and women here in town."

"My fear, too, Eddie. I'll let you know if I can find out any more information on that text message from the other day."

"Frankie, wait. I got another one. This one isn't a threat. It's a direct warning and aimed at Darcy."

Frankie studied the message, then stared at the wall behind Eddie, sudden knowledge causing fear to rise. He handed Eddie his phone.

"Send me that. I think Darcy's a smoke screen, to pull our attention away from something else. What big festivals do we have coming up?"

Eddie's fingers froze on his phone keyboard as it hit him what Frankie was saying. "You're not saying what I think you're saying?"

Frankie nodded. "I'll be back in a bit. Go find Caleb and get his thoughts."

Chapter 23

Caleb stared at Eddie. "Is he serious?"

Eddie nodded. "I think he's on to something. This going after Darcy never seemed to fit with what was happening around us. This makes more sense."

Caleb looked down at the map he had drawn while Eddie was talking. "You're right, it does. Frankie's figured out what has puzzled us. Now how do we deal with this? This is right in our own town."

Eddie nodded. "And we have to do it in such a way that word doesn't leak out. Who do you want in on the meeting, where and when?"

"You, Frankie, Doug, EMS chief, fire chief, search and rescue head. We need to keep it small, that way word doesn't get out." Caleb turned to his calendar. "I'm freeing up my day. Do the same. Start making the calls and arrange a place for us to meet. Bring Ben in on this as a consultant."

Eddie stood. "Say some prayers, Caleb. I have a feeling Frankie's right and this festival next week is the actual target."

Caleb nodded. "It's one of the biggest draws in the area. We need to head off whatever it is before he strikes." He searched his desk and pulled out a folder. "Here, Jace came through with more. Work it into our plans. He was getting the same vibes as Frankie."

Doug looked around at the men seated at the conference table in the fire hall board room. They all looked puzzled as to the meeting called on short notice.

Caleb finally stood at the end. "Men, we have new information on the situation around us. Speculation has been rampant that Darcy O'Shaughnessy has been the cause of it all. True, she has been targeted but as a smoke screen to the real target. Our Harvest Festival that's coming up? That's the real target." Caleb waited for the murmurs to die down. "That's why I've called the meeting with just us few. We need to make plans, but we need to keep this as quiet as we can to prevent panic."

"How do we do that?" The fire chief stared down the table at Caleb, fingers tapping on the table top.

"That's what this meeting is for, to brainstorm and come up with plans."

"So, what do we know already?" The EMS supervisor spoke up.

Caleb passed over the information they had accrued. The faces of the men grew more somber and stern as they read.

"This guy is sick. How do we stop him?" was the consensus as they finished reading.

Ideas flew around the table and became concrete. Doug sat back, listening, getting the full picture, not just the snippet regarding Darcy and his heart chilled. They were right, this guy needed to be stopped. Could they do it in time was the question?

Caleb looked at the clock. "Okay, let's finish up. Get working on the plans for your own service. We meet again in two days, same time. Here is okay with everyone?"

Doug paused by Eddie as they waited to leave the room. "How does Darcy now fit into this?"

"As a smokescreen, Doug, in part. I think he's after her for what happened in college, and has used that to cover what he's really up to."

"I hate to ask, but Darcy mentioned a name."

Eddie didn't speak, just stared at Doug.

Doug nodded. "That's what I figured. I'll warn her to watch more carefully."

"You can warn all you want, Doug. We could be around her all the time, and he could still get to her. He proved that today. There's no doubt in my mind the two are connected."

Doug sighed. "I know and that scares me. We have no idea where or when he'll strike, even if we're right about next week."

Eddie agreed. "We can't shut down the festival. We can't lock up the town and the inhabitants and keep everyone else out. We have to plan and take what steps we can.

Caleb's putting out requests for extra officers from other towns and cities to come in. They all realize what the potential is for something to happen."

Doug pulled up to Darcy's home later that afternoon. He knew she was home. He stepped from his truck, eyes searching the area around and going beyond to her neighbours. Where is he, Lord? Is he here that I can get him?

Darcy stood on the steps and watched Doug. He looked up and a smile crossed his face. They had no real plans but he knew he would have to talk to her about what they had discovered.

"So, he's not really after me at all then?"

"That's not what we're saying, Darcy. He is after you, or some else is, who we figure is his son. You're the smokescreen to what he is planning next week during the festival."

"That's a horrible thought," she responded. "All those people here. Where would he plant his bombs?"

"That's what we're trying to determine. What would be your thoughts?"

She rose from where she had been sitting next to him on the couch and paced, deep in thought. He watched as she struggled to think like the maniac as he called him thought.

She turned. "The football field. The library. The furthest fire or EMS station. The bank at the other end of town. Now for downtown, Mac's would be one place I would think should be watched. The department building is another. He's not going to care who he hurts or how many. It's about making a statement now. He's gone too far to pull back, even if he wanted to." Her eyes still stared into the distance. "He will use this younger man in a way you would never expect him too, and he really doesn't care if he dies or not."

She finally turned to Doug. "Have I given you enough?"

"Too much, Darcy. Now, how do you think he will set the bombs?"

"Bombs. Yes, he will use those again. Timers. Cell phone triggers. Whatever means he can use to set them off he will. It's going to be difficult to defuse them unless we prevent him from setting them. The only way to do that is to make sure the police presence is felt in a big way. How much overtime is Caleb authorizing?"

"I would say a lot. He's asking for officers from outside the town."

"Does he need me to meet with anyone over the next few days?"

"He hasn't said. I think he wants to keep you out of it as much as possible."

She nodded, then sat down beside him again, rubbing her arms against a sudden chill.

"This scares me, Doug. How do we prevent a massive incident?"

"I don't know that we can humanly, Darcy, but God can. He's used you so far, and now He's using Caleb. We need to keep our prayers going."

She leant against him. "Why did it have to be me, Doug? Someone else would have suited me to a T."

"I know, sweetheart, but He chose you. Let Him work through you, okay?"

She sighed. "I have no choice, now do I?"

Chapter 24

Caleb stood and watched as the crowds grew day by day leading up to the festival. Plans were in place to try and counteract what they knew was coming, but without definite targets, they could only plan so much. Bill Watson had been in touch, wanting to know how the investigation was going from Caleb's point of view. Caleb could tell he was digging for information. Without his suspicions, Caleb would never have known, just by the way the questions were framed.

Doug stood beside him, eyes searching the crowds, stopping every once in a while to really study a pedestrian.

"It looks as if the crowds are bigger this year."

"I think you're right. For this early in the festival, I would say they are. That makes it so much more interesting, now doesn't it?"

"Smiles, Caleb. Keep that smile on your face, you're always telling me. I know what you're saying though. This makes it tough. Our plans are all ready?"

"As much as they can be. I don't like this not knowing, nor do any of the other leaders. They're on edge, and the men are picking up on that, wondering what they haven't been told."

"And we couldn't tell them. I think it's time we did though, so they're aware of what's coming."

Caleb sighed. "That's what the consensus was at our meeting this morning. They'll be talking to their people today, preparing them."

"Darcy's taken to hiding in the back of her store if she can. Abby's helping out any way when she can."

"Abby's been a blessing to her. She'll be missed on the force when she leaves."

"She will be." Doug turned as Tom came towards him.

"Have you seen this yet, Doug?" He handed him his phone. "He's working out from you leaders to the men now."

Caleb looked over Doug's shoulder as he read. "He's not threatening Darcy this time. He's threatening the town. Doing it this way, he's spreading fear among the masses, or trying to. Tom, see if you can find out who has received a message like this, within our service and any other emergency service. We need to start drawing our people in closer to the heart of the matter, and let them know we are looking for two men and two men only. We have confirmation that Bill Watson is one of them. Another man by the name of Joe Whitson is the other. Circulate Whitson's picture only for now. I'm working on a way to try and draw Watson out."

"Bill Watson, as in Chief Watson?" Tom was dumbfounded.

"That goes no further, Tom. We can't blow our cover with him and alert him to the fact that we're looking for him."

Tom nodded. "I'll get the picture of Whitson circulating. I still can't believe it."

Doug watched Tom walk away, then turned to Caleb. "It's official now?"

Caleb sighed. "It is. And whatever he's planning, it will be within the next day or so from what my sources say. I just wish they had come forward before."

"They never do, Caleb, unless we're out there poking and prodding, and even then, there's no guarantee they will talk."

Darcy watched as Doug walked towards her. She saw the fatigue in his steps.

"Doug, what are you doing here?"

He smiled. "I just wanted to see my girl. Something wrong with that?"

She shook her head. "No. I'm glad to see you. I just wasn't expecting to see you in the middle of the day. You have news?"

He nodded and extended his hands. "Can you walk with me for a bit?"

"Let me grab my jacket and let Abby know."

He grasped her hand tight in his and led her away from the downtown area, mingling with the crowds.

"What can you tell me?" Darcy's eyes roamed the crowds.

"The person you suspected has been confirmed. We are also looking for the son."

"So, it is his son?"

Doug nodded. "It is. He's never acknowledged him as such. The son doesn't know that's his father who's been using him."

"That's so sad, Doug. The whole situation could likely have been avoided years ago if different decisions had been made back then."

Doug agreed.

"So, what do we do now?"

"For now, we wait. We've got plans in place to deal with what we figure will happen, but until we know for sure, we can't do anything."

Darcy squeezed his hand. "I know. Patience is not easy in situations like this."

Doug stopped, staring ahead of him. "Darcy, that man just ahead of us. Do you recognize him?"

"Which one?" Her hand gripped harder. "It's him, the one from the group."

"That's what I thought. Listen, he doesn't seem to know we're here. I'm taking a chance with you here, but this is what we're going to do. We're going to walk up to him and speak with him. You stay back a bit. I'll stay between you and see if I can get him to come with us."

It worked exactly as Doug had wanted. The young man turned and walked back with them towards the department. Darcy frowned as she studied him. Something wasn't right, she thought. He's not acting normal, not like he did all those years ago. What has happened to him in the meantime?

Doug delivered his charge to the booking officer, then taking Darcy's hand again, went in search of Caleb. He found Caleb, Eddie and Frankie together in Caleb's office, going over plans.

Caleb looked up in surprise to see the two. "What's wrong, Doug?"

"Nothing too much, Caleb. Darcy and I had gone for a walk through the crowds and spotted one of our suspects ahead of us. He's in custody."

"Whitson?"

Doug nodded. "I just approached him, called him by name, asked him to come with me and he did. It was so strange. He didn't resist at all."

"There's something wrong with him, Caleb." Darcy spoke up. "I think you need to have him evaluated. I'm not sure if there's something physical or mental or even organic that's wrong. He needs help."

Frankie stared at her. "He's threatened you and you want to help him?"

Darcy spun at him. "Do we have concrete evidence it was him? Do we?" When he couldn't respond, she continued, "We don't, do we? Even if we did, I would still ask for help for him. He needs it. He is a human being. We don't know for sure if he was involved in any of the incidents that happened. My feeling and assessment is that he wasn't but was set up as the fall guy.

Now you prove me wrong." At that, she spun and almost ran from the office.

The four men stared after her, not quite sure what to do.

"Well, I guess you were told." Eddie's droll voice broke the silence. "Now, go do what she asked. Prove her right or wrong."

Franke shook his head and glared at Doug. "See what she's got me doing now, more digging."

Doug laughed. "She's good at that, and she's usually right when she says something like that. And before you ask I have no way of knowing how she does it."

Caleb shook his head at their nonsense, then turned back to his plans. "Are we clear as to what we're looking for?"

Frankie nodded. "We are. We've brought in extra bomb detection dogs, extra crews. I just pray we're right and we're not leaving another town open to attack."

"I don't think we are. It has always revolved around this town. I can't figure out why though. He's never lived here as far as I can tell, has no connection to us."

"There has to be something," Eddie muttered. "Ben hasn't said anything and if he knew, he would tell us."

Caleb's phone rang at that moment. When he answered it, he was surprised to hear his wife, Hannah's, voice. He sat down as he listened to her and his eyes slid shut. The other men froze in place as they watched his reaction, Eddie nodding.

When Caleb had slowly laid his phone back on the table, Eddie spoke. "Hannah just gave you a name, didn't she?"

Caleb looked up and nodded. "She did. I prayed the Lord wouldn't do this to her this time. I have never been able to figure out how she knows, except He gives the names to her." He looked up, eyes stricken with remorse. "She really didn't want to give me the name. Do any of you recognize the name, Robert Beckett?"

Frankie and Doug shook their heads in the negative. Eddie stared at Caleb, then nodded. "There's your connection, Caleb. I remember now I hear the name. Bill Watson had a hunting buddy who was a judge here in town. Robert Beckett. That's how he would have gotten those documents past the background search. I always heard rumours about him when I worked the streets."

"Is he still in town?"

"For part of the year. He spends about four months of the year on an island somewhere in the south. He's out of town right now."

"Is he just a hunting buddy or closer?" Doug's quiet question hung in the air.

"What are you asking, Doug?" Eddie had an idea of where Doug was going with that.

"Who is Whitson's mother? I don't think we've ever said. Do we know?" Doug's eyes moved from man to man.

Caleb sat back in his chair, eyes on Doug. "I don't think we ever did. Frankie, do we know?"

Frankie reached for the folder he had laid down with the statistics on Whitson. "It says here her last name is…." His voice died away. "Did we never follow up on that? I don't remember seeing anything come back on her."

"What's the name?" Caleb prodded for Frankie to speak.

"It's Beckett, and what'll you want to bet it's a female relative of Beckett."

"Find out who was looking up that information. I want to talk to them today." Caleb's voice was tight. "I know it wasn't you or Eddie, Frankie. This would never have gotten by you. This could have stopped all this earlier."

Frankie nodded as he flew from the room to track down the officer responsible. He would not want to be in that person's shoes right now.

Chapter 25

Caleb sighed as he shut his door. Apologies for missing information that had cost so much really didn't cut it, he thought. No, that officer would be going back to patrol, if they chose to stay with the force, and that wasn't likely.   A good officer brought down by an oversight. Never good, he thought.

He reached for his phone and then changed his mind and reached for his Bible instead. He needed wisdom in the next day or so and only God's wisdom and comfort would do.   He knew his officers and his friends had asked their family members to stay away for areas in town, including the downtown area.   Whatever the crisis that was coming, it was coming fast. They could all feel it.

He reached for his phone to access his messages.   He blinked at the number of them from Bill Watson. He shuddered as he listened to the last one, Bill's voice barely containing a rage.   He was at the line and ready to cross over for a final time, Caleb thought, and they just didn't have the evidence they needed to prevent it.

A knock came to his door, and Eddie entered.

"I spoke with Myra Beckett, Robert's daughter. She admitted that Whitson is her son and that Bill Watson is the father. An unwanted pregnancy is how she termed it. She doesn't have a good word to say about him, even after all these years."

"I didn't think she did. She's still in town?"

Eddie shook his head. "No, she moved from here before Whitson was born. She has no contact with her family, feels that they betrayed her. She didn't go into a lot of details and I didn't ask, but there's a lot of bitterness and hatred there."

"And it's coming through the son towards others." Caleb thought through the interview with Whitson he had read. "Darcy was right. This fellow does need a lot of help. It's like he's been driven to act by forces from without."

"I have a team going through his apartment. They're finding interesting technical devices that he denies ever seeing. I think his mind's been played with."

"That is has, Eddie. Now are we all set for tomorrow?"

Eddie nodded. "As much as we can be. You've set the trap?"

"I have. Listen to this last voice mail from him. He's about gone over the edge."

Eddie listened, then asked Caleb to replay it. "Did you hear that in the background?"

"I caught something. What is it?"

"It's the clock in the town hall. He's already in town."

The two men looked at each other. Caleb stood. "Grab the men we designated and start searching today. If he's here, he'll likely already be planting his devices."

"I was afraid of that, Caleb. We're on it. You'll be in touch with the others?"

Caleb was reaching for his phone as he nodded. "On it."

Doug looked up as Eddie stopped in his doorway.

"Today, Doug. He's in town. We're searching today."

Doug was out of his chair and heading for his team. "Where do you want us?"

"The high school for now. I've got word out for a lock down at all the schools. The principals are aware of what's happening and have released the statement we've prepared. As far as anyone is concerned, we're working a training exercise and need the schools to go through a practice drill too. We had had them send a letter to the parents to expect this in the next few weeks, so there won't be any surprise."

"We'll be there."

Darcy stood at her store window, watching the crowds moving by. Her store was almost at capacity with customers, and she and Abby had not had a chance to catch their breath since the store opened. She watched down the street as teams moved from the department building. Was it today, Lord? Will it be all over today?

She turned as someone touched her shoulder. Mac stood there, grin in place.

"I didn't think you two ladies would be getting away for your lunch." He held up a bag with carryout packages in it. "It's just sandwiches and salads and SuEllen threw in some snack stuff for you. I'll leave it in your fridge at the back."

Darcy reached out to hug him. "Thank you, Mac. You look after everyone in town. How do you do it?"

He shrugged, grin still in place. "When we started the cafe, we asked the Lord to bless it and to help us expand to those in need around us. He has blessed us in ways we never imagined. This is our mission field, Darcy, this town."

"Thank you again, Mac. Here, I'll take that. I know you're swamped at the cafe."

He watched her for a minute. "Does Doug know the treasure he has in you?"

She stared at him, mouth open, as he laughed and moved away from her through the crowds. She stopped by Abby at the counter and held up the bag.

"Lunch or whatever you want to call it, Abby. Mac's been by."

"Oh, good. You grab something first, then I will. I don't believe how busy we've been."

"I know. And that scares me, Abby, knowing he's out there somewhere."

Abby sobered. "I know. The teams are out looking for him. Pray they find him."

"That's been a constant with me for weeks now, Abby. I just need this over with."

Doug shook his head as he watched the bomb squad dismantle a bomb in the library. They had cleared it when word came in about a suspicious package.

"Darcy was right about this place."

Frankie turned to him. "She was. I'm afraid everywhere she said, we'll find a bomb. People will be saying she's working with him."

"I know. We'll have to have the PR people bring out a strong statement when it's over, making it clear she was a victim too."

"They're already working on that. Caleb set them to that last week. Once this is over, the statement comes out. Then you two can go on with your lives."

Doug slanted him a glance. "Us and everyone else in the area. So much has been put on hold because of one person." He turned as Tom approached.

"They've found another two, Frankie, right where Darcy had said. How did she know, Doug?"

"She studies the culprit and somehow can think like he does to a certain extent. Then she looks around where he's planning to exploit and figures it out. She's good at that. When she quit working as a forensics psychologist, the emergency forces lost someone they shouldn't have. She's adamant this is her last. She won't do it again."

"And that's a real shame. She's excellent at what she does." Frankie turned as the bomb squad leader approached.

"What do we have, Adam?"

"Well, let's put it this way. He's good but we're better. His bombs are not the same as what he had set off. He's getting sloppy. And getting sloppy is going to hurt us."

Frankie nodded. "He's running scared and knows this is it for him."

Adam gave him a sour look. "I would like to get my hands on him. We've lost too many good people to him. If he's in law enforcement, he needs to get out and pay for his crimes. And I would say he's in law enforcement."

"Why would you say that, Adam?" Doug spoke up.

"He's using material not available to the general public, unless he's getting them on the black market. And that's scary. We don't know what we're going to find with any of these. This one was set to go off at 8:00 a.m. tomorrow, right when the parade was gathering outside the doors."

Frankie's face whitened and he shot a look at Doug. "I'll pass that on to Caleb. It's what we were figuring he would be doing."

Adam stared at Frankie. "I have a feeling Caleb's keeping something really close about this guy. Tell him for me to catch him and find out where all the bombs are so we can disarm them. And Doug, I understand your lady has helped. Thank her for us, will you?"

Doug stared, stunned that the word had gotten out. "How did you know?"

Adam grinned. "We know what she used to do and how good she is. When word started coming through about where to look, we knew it was her."

Caleb looked around as he stood outside the high school. "Where exactly did they find the bomb?"

"Under the bleachers, set to go off during the game tomorrow." Eddie stood beside him, stance rigid.

Caleb's face tightened with anger. "During the game? This guy is sick, Eddie."

"He is and now I wonder if he is even working on his own. There's just something odd about these ones. Someone knows our town too well for these to be chance placements. Darcy has pretty much nailed where they'll be. Doug mentioned that Adam from the bomb squad said to thank her, that when word came through where to find the bombs and knowing she lives in town, they knew it was her letting them know where to find them.   Doug was shocked, I think, to hear that."

Caleb nodded. "We've kept her name out of it as much as we can, but she's well known in the emergency services for what she's done in the past. She's one of the best. I'm sorry to see her retire from it."

"We've found a number of bombs already. Adam says they're scary."

"I imagine they are.   Does he think we've found them all?"

"He won't say. I somehow don't think we have."

"I don't either.   I'm heading back to the department.   Let's hope Bill Watson hasn't tracked me down." He looked at his phone and groaned. "And he has."

"He's here?"

Caleb nodded.   "And wants to meet with me. I have meetings all morning with our guys and the town council. There's no way I can meet with him today at all." He sent a message to his secretary. "It's better

if I don't.   I don't know if I could keep it
quiet."

Chapter 26

Caleb looked up from the paperwork inundating his desk to see Adam in his doorway.

"Adam, come in. Shut the door."

Adam looked fatigued. "I think we've found them all, Caleb, but I can't be certain. It was a brutal day. I don't know who this guy is, but he's dangerous."

"I know who he is and we're not saying yet. But you're right, he is dangerous and he is in law enforcement."

Adam shook his head. "I don't understand why."

"We don't have all the answers yet, but we're working on it. We think tomorrow's the day he had it all planned for, and you certainly have confirmed that with the bombs. I just pray we've found them all."

"There are just too many buildings to sweep properly, especially with the crowds in town. He knows that. I have a fear we've missed one that will take out a number of people."

"You've done the best you can, Adam. Go home and get some sleep. It's going to be an early day and a long day tomorrow."

Adam nodded as he rose. "You need to get out of here too, Caleb."

Caleb shook his head. "I'll be spending the night here. It won't be the first time."

"Nor the last."

Morning came too early, Doug thought, as he rolled over to squint at his clock. It was 4 a.m. and he had to be at the department in thirty minutes. He groaned as he pushed himself up and out of bed. Lord, let it all be finished today. Keep everyone safe. Let Adam and the teams have found all the bombs. And please, Lord, keep my lady safe. He'll go after her today when the bombs don't go off.

Darcy turned as Doug walked through the door, just after she had opened the store. He motioned to the back and she followed him, to walk into his arms as he stopped and turned.

"What is it, Doug?"

He shrugged. "I just needed to see you and give you a hug." He leaned back to look down at her upturned face. "I didn't get a chance to see you yesterday, it was so busy."

Darcy studied his face. "Did you find them all?"

"We pray we did. Everywhere you said there'd be one, we found one. Adam from the bomb squad said to thank you."

"How did he know? I thought Caleb was keeping my name out of it."

Doug hugged her even tighter. "He did. It's just that this forensics psychologist I happen to know was very good at her job and word got around. When they realized they were finding the bombs where they were told, without having the suspect in custody, they knew it was you." He dropped a kiss on her lips as he stepped back. "I have to go. Stay close to Abby, okay? He'll be after you when he realizes the bombs aren't going off."

She nodded, a thought crossing her mind.

"And no, don't put yourself out there, Darcy. I couldn't stand to lose you again now that I've found you."

Darcy shook her head at him. "I won't deliberately do that, you know that, Doug. But if it means saving others, what would you have me to do?"

He reached to caress her cheek. "I guess I would say, do what God leads you to. I just want you in my life for a long time, that's all I'm saying."

Darcy stood and watched him walk away from her. Doug, you know that I won't stand by and see others hurt. It's not in me any more to do that. Nor is it in you.

Darcy turned mid-morning from helping a customer to see Ian standing behind her.

"Ian! This is a pleasant surprise. What are you shopping for?"

He shook his head. "We're not shopping. We're here to be with you today. Any reaching or lifting let us know."

"You and who else?"

"Matt.   He's over there by the counter."

She looked past him. "Matt. And Sarah. Yes, she's one I need to meet. Come introduce me, then tell me why you're really here."

Matt watched as Ian walked towards him with an auburn-haired lady. That has to be Darcy, he thought.

"Matt, this is Darcy O'Shaughnessy, owner of this store, and Doug's lady."

Darcy extended her hand. "Hi. And I want to meet your Sarah."

"Sarah?"   Matt was puzzled and looked towards Ian, who had started to grin.

"Yes, your Sarah. Is that a problem?"

"Ah, no." Matt again looked at Ian.

"Ian, you didn't explain that to her? Shame on you." Darcy shook her head as she walked away to assist a customer.

"Ian."   Matt's eyes narrowed as he looked at a grinning Ian.

"You weren't in our vehicle the day we took them to that meeting. Abe just happened to mention that most of the ladies we were to protect ended up running. Darcy decided she needs to meet them, find out their technique and refine it."

Ian jumped as Darcy's voice came from behind him. "Not just refine it. I've been looking for a theme for my master's thesis. This is just perfect."

"Do you always sneak up on people?" Ian turned to her.

She grinned at him. "No, I didn't. Matt saw me."

Ian shook his head. "Where would you like us?"

"Do I have a choice?"

Both men shook their heads. "Abe sent us in to be with you today. I don't suppose any one told you that Doug and Abe are cousins?" Ian grinned at the expression on her face.

"No, they didn't." She stopped, then looked at them in delight. "That means Rebecca will be a cousin. Oh, this just gets better and better." She spun and walked away from them.

"Is she for real?" Matt couldn't help asking, as Ian started to laugh.

Doug looked around the building they were searching. "Anything, Tom?"

"No, there isn't. He didn't come back here. I wonder if he did plant any more, or if we've missed them." He looked at Doug. "Do you suppose he knew we'd find them and this was just a diversion tactic?"

Doug froze, then turned to Tom. "Now, I wonder if we even considered that. I'm sure we did. Has anyone see Bill Watson today?"

Tom shook his head. "He's the one person no one has seen in a day or so. We tried to reach him at his office, and his secretary said he was called out of town on a personal emergency."

"Personal emergency. That fits with what we've been getting from him." Doug looked around. "If we're done here, let's move to the next building on our list. Any word from the other teams?"

"They're all coming up blank too. It's too bizarre, Doug. Where is he?"

Standing by his cruiser, Caleb searched the crowds. Watson was here somewhere, he was certain. But where? He turned as he heard his name called. Jace was running towards him.

"I just got new information in, Caleb. It's not good. Whitson's mother is in town and we found out that Beckett left his home down on the islands today. We're tracing his flight now to see where it lands. It's a private jet."

Caleb turned to look for Eddie and waved him over. He relayed the information that Jace had just given him.

Eddie shook his head. "Of course she would be, and of course Beckett would be headed here. I'll put out the word, Caleb, and get pictures out to the patrol officers."

"I just hope we're in time, Eddie, to prevent something from happening."

Chapter 27

Doug turned as he heard his name called.

"Doug, watch your back. We have the others in town now." Caleb gaze was constantly moving, searching through the crowds.

"Do we have photos?"

"They're sending them out now. Watch for a text message from the office. All clear's where you've been?"

"It is. We're moving towards the centre of town more now. So far, it's all been clear."

"I don't like that, Doug. I would have thought he would plant more."

"Tom thinks the bombs were a diversionary tactic."

Caleb shot him a keen glance. "I have a feeling he's right." Caleb turned to walk away. "Who's with Darcy?"

"Abby, and Abe sent in Ian and Matt. His other men are around in the crowd."

Doug turned as Tom came back up to him, shaking his head.

"There are no more bombs, Doug. So, what kind of game is he playing?"

"I wish I knew, Tom. This is far from over. We're all being sent a text message with two more faces to watch for."

"Two?"

"That's right. And I have no idea what their participation in all of this is."

The men turned to scan the crowds, fear growing within them as they saw the volume of people. This could go bad very quickly. They then walked towards the centre of town, eyes constantly on the move.

A sudden cry of "He's got a gun" rang through the crowds. Doug and Tom fought their way through the running pedestrians, searching to find the gunman. They heard the chatter over their radios and turned towards the high school.

"Foster!" Doug started to turn as he heard his name called, then spun and went down. Tom dropped beside him.

"Do you see him?" Tom asked.

Doug shook his head, hand clamped to his left upper arm. "I didn't. Did you?"

Tom shook his head, then sensing something wrong, turned to Doug. "He got you?"

Doug nodded. "Winged me. Let's move." He was on his feet and moving again before Tom could respond.

"Where'd he go?" Tom searched the crowds that remained, huddled on the ground.

"I don't see him. Dispatch, we have an active shooter near the high school." Doug's voice rang through the radio. "Send backup but ensure our targets are still covered."

Doug's thoughts flew for a moment to Darcy and he prayed for her safety before he concentrated once again on finding the shooter.

"Was it Watson?" Tom's voice was soft beside him.

"I don't know but I'm sure it was."

Darcy turned once again as Ian approached her.

"Have you had your lunch yet, Darcy?"

She shook her head. "I sent Abby but haven't had a chance myself."

He nodded towards the back. "Matt's willing to help where he can while you grab a bite."

She sank gratefully into a chair. "I didn't realize it would be so busy."

Ian sat across from her. "It always is with this festival. It's your first one here, isn't it?"

She nodded. "It is. I'll have to plan better next year." She looked at Ian. "Tell me, why do you do what you do?"

"Be in security?" At her nod, he shrugged. "It's something that's always interested me and when Abe offered me a chance to work with him, I took it. Why did you become a forensics psychologist?"

She had to think about that one, then with a small smile, she replied, "I guess back when I was deciding on a major in college, I wanted something different. You know how it says that the devil is like a roaring lion walking around? I wanted to help defeat him and this is one way I could."

"That's an interesting perspective to bring to a job." Ian studied her. "Where does Doug fit in?"

She smiled. "Somehow, I knew that was coming. I've had time to think about it over the years. One thing that attracted me when we first met was that he took care of everyone. He likes to joke and tease, but he's one you can depend on any time you need someone. He reminds me of a lion pacing through the wilds of Africa, on alert even when asleep, ready to attack and defend. He has that heart, Ian, if you can catch what I'm saying."

Ian nodded. "He does. I've gotten to know him over the last few years, and that's exactly how he is." He looked up as a sound came at the back door. "Are you expecting a delivery today?"

She shook her head. "No, I'm not. No, Ian, don't go there, please."

Ian motioned for her to stay where she was and moved silently to the door. Listening he could hear nothing.

"Darcy, come back out front with Matt. I'm going around to check it. Where are your keys for the door?" He took them as she handed them over. "Don't leave Matt's side. Let him know where I am."

Darcy watched in apprehension as he moved out the front of the store and she could see his form moving past the front windows.

Ian walked in from the back, shaking his head. There was nothing there now, but he knew he had heard something. He needed Darcy to clear the store; his feelings were something was about to happen.

"Darcy, we need you to clear the store, if you can. There was nothing there now, but someone was. I could see fresh scratch marks around the lock." Ian looked over at Matt, who nodded. "Can we come up with an excuse, but keep the customers happy?"

"Let me think for a minute. This is tough, Ian. What kind of excuse can I make that's legitimate?"

Ian held up a finger as he answered his phone, eyes tracking between Matt and Darcy. As he slid his phone back into his pocket, he hesitated, knowing it would it would be hard for Darcy to close her shop.

"Matt, Darcy, that was Caleb. We have an active shooter in the downtown area, over a few blocks. They're asking all merchants to close down for now until they can clear the area. Police officers will be moving the people through the area and out to safety."

Darcy nodded, then turned to Matt. "Matt, can you help? If we can get people's names and phone numbers as they're leaving, we can get in touch with them and offer them compensation of some kind."

Matt headed for the door, paper and pen in hand. Ian stayed near the back watching as Darcy and Abby managed to clear the store in short order. Abby was sent on her way.

Matt locked the door and then turned to Darcy. "Now what do we need to do to get you out of here?"

She turned to the cash register. "I just need a few minutes to close this off and then I can put the receipts in the safe. Ten minutes, max, I think."

Tom finally pulled Doug to a stop. "Let me look at that arm. You're still bleeding."

Doug tried to shrug off his hand. "It will be all right."

"Doug, if it was one of us, you'd have the paramedics looking at us. At least let me wrap something around it for now. We need you functioning, not flat on your back."

Doug leaned back against the wall he was near. "You're right, Tom. Here, wrap this around it."

"A handkerchief, Doug?"

Doug nodded, with a small smile. "Talk to Caleb about that. He's got all his friends carrying them. He says we need them for ladies in distress. Cloth is better to offer them than a paper tissue, he tells me."

Tom gave a low laugh as he tightened the knot. "He may have something there. No sign of our shooter. Where's he headed?"

"I have no idea. I didn't see him in the first place, did you?"

"No. I just heard the yells and then saw you hit. Come to think of it, I never heard a shot."

"Silencer then. Come on. We need to keep searching." He stopped. "Where're Eddie and Frankie?"

"Where they need to be. Now lead on."

Bill Watson stood and watched from the shadows as Doug and Tom moved away from him. He had missed taking out Doug. Weapon raised, he steadied his aim on Doug, tightened his finger on the trigger, then lowered his weapon again. No, there was a better way to get back at him. He turned, scanning for other officers, then sank back into the darkness of the alley. He would head back to where he had just been. He had watched as Ian had searched the area, and then gone back inside. He knew he could get in now. She would be his to exact his revenge on. That would be revenge on Doug, hurting his lady.

Ian stood behind Darcy as she shut the safe and make sure it was locked, then closed the cupboard door that hid it. He sensed a motion behind him. As he turned, a heavy blow hit him in the back and he stumbled forward, arms sweeping out to take Darcy to the floor, a shout dying on his lips before he could sound it. Darcy gave a small scream as she hit the floor, breath knocked from her, Ian's body covering hers in a protective manner.

She heard voices, then Ian was roughly dragged from her and dropped to the floor, to lay motionless. Her wrist was grabbed and she was pulled ruthlessly to her feet and shoved up again a wall, weapon to her temple. Vision slowly clearing, she could see Matt, hands in the air, standing in the doorway to the store.

A voice snarled in her ear, but she couldn't understand the words. The weapon pressed in harder, then it was released and she was pulled roughly from the wall and shoved to the centre of the room. Spinning, she faced her nemesis.

"I should have known it would be you, Bill Watson. What did I ever do to you?"

She watched as his visage changed, to become a snarling mask of dislike and rage.

"You ask that? You ask THAT?" he yelled. "How dare you?" Gun raised to hit her, he stepped towards her, then retreated. Not yet, he thought, not yet. She has to suffer and so do those two with her.

"Yes, I do dare to ask that. What did I ever do to you?"

He spit at her in his rage, just missing her face. "I'll tell you what you did. You've haunted me for years. You've ruined my life, is what you've done."

"What do you mean, haunted you for years?"

"Yes, years. Whitson is my son and you chased him from your group and from the college."

"Whitson? Your son? You never let on, all the time you tried to get into a leadership or mentorship role with our group. You were there the night we all decided he had to leave. I wasn't the one who made the motion. I never agreed or disagreed with it."

"Neutral." He snorted, sounding like an angry bull. "Neutral. That is still a decision against him."

Darcy shook her head. "No, Bill. It wasn't. I didn't have enough facts to make a decision, and no one else wanted to learn any more. If you had listened you would have heard them asking Whitson for more but you have chosen to ignore that fact. Being your son wouldn't have made any difference."

He paced in front of her, agitation driving him. "It would have."

"No, it wouldn't have. And you know that. He's the reason all those seniors died before I was called in. How did he ever get to be on the force anyway?"

He glared at her in anger. "I have a friend who helped get him there. You're the reason he had to leave."

"No, he did that to himself. Or rather, you did, creating a false identity and resume for him. Did you really think he would not get caught out at some time?"

Watson strode away from her, stared down at the still form of Ian, and then stared past her at Matt. He no longer had control. She was taking over. Weapon raised, he walked towards her once again.

"You deserve to die for what you did."

She shook her head, calmness and peace flowing through her. "No, I don't but you do. You have killed so many, Bill. How many others over the years have you removed from your life or Whitson's life?"

He stared at her. How did she know? It was like she was reading his mind. Hand to his head, he waved his weapon. "Stop. You can't know that."

"So, you are admitting, in front of witnesses, that you have killed before? How many, Bill? How many families have you destroyed over the years? What happened to make you do that?" Darcy kept pressing him, looking for answers. She caught a whisper of movement behind him. Someone was in the back room, listening. Lord, this is it. We need to finish this before he kills again. But how do we do that? He'll want to be leaving, and I know he'll want me to go with him, but Lord, I just can't do that. I can't leave these two men, and I can't let him hurt them either.

"You're coming with me, Darcy. You're my ticket out of here."

She shook her head. "No, I'm not leaving. I won't be party to any more of your decisions or leading. I'm done." She took a step backwards towards Matt. "You can turn around and walk away. I won't call for fifteen minutes. That will give you time to get away."

He shook his head and paced again. She could see his visage changing again and was suddenly afraid. Has she pushed too hard? Lord, I need Your protection. So do Ian and Matt. Send in Your angels, Lord. She took another step backwards, seeing a slight movement from Ian. He was alive, thank You, Lord. Now to keep them alive.

Watson turned and stared at her, an empty look in his eyes now. "No, you're coming with me. They won't hurt me if I take you." He reached suddenly and caught her wrist in an iron grip and pulled her forward. She struggled against him, twisting her arm until she broke free.

The whisper of movement in the back room came again. Frankie moved to the doorway, weapon raised.

"Drop the weapon and raise your hands, Watson.   You're under arrest for murder."

Watson kept his eyes glued to Darcy. "Not a chance of that, Brennan. Get out of here.   I'm arresting her for being an accomplice to the bomber."

Frankie shook his head. "No, Watson. Now drop the weapon and put your hands up."

Watson turned his head to look at Frankie, then spun back to face Darcy. His weapon never wavered from her as his finger found the trigger.   As his weapon discharged, a shot sounded from behind Frankie, from the shelter of the back room. Watson dropped to the floor, weapon spinning away from him.   Frankie moved from the back room and kicked the weapon away even further, then stooped to check for a pulse, his own weapon not discharged. A cry from Matt raised his head.

Darcy lay motionless on the floor, Matt bending over her.

"Frankie, we need something to stop the bleeding. He hit her in the chest."

Frankie froze, then turned to rummage through the cupboards.

"Here, take these towels." He reached for his radio, then thought better. "Can you manage for a minute?"

Matt nodded. "Get help. I'm trying to stop the bleeding but we need to get her to a trauma centre. Ian, you're on your feet. Good. I need your help here."

Ian stumbled to where Darcy lay and dropped to his knees. "What do you need?"

"Here, press on these. We need to keep the pressure on it. I have to check for her vitals. Frankie's gone for help."

Town paramedics converged to help. Matt took over again from Ian, keeping the pressure on the wound.

"Stay off the radio, guys, until we can find Doug." The paramedics looked up at him, not understanding what he was saying. "This is Lieutenant Doug Foster's fiancee. I don't want him hearing anything over the radio." He turned to an officer. "Find the chief and get him to me."

"We have a LifeFlight chopper just a couple of streets over. Caleb had it on standby."

"Good. Your ambulance is out front?"

They nodded.

"Okay, so how do you want to do this?"

"Backboard, then stretcher. Matt, keep that pressure on that wound. You'll be in an awkward position but you're going to have to manage. You'll be on the flight with them."

Caleb pushed through the door, and stood by Frankie. "I heard you needed me."

Frankie nodded. "Watson's dead, but he got Darcy before I got him. He moved so fast I didn't get to him in time. Someone was behind me, Caleb, and shot him."

"How bad?"

The lead paramedic looked up. "It's touch and go, Caleb. If someone hadn't reacted right away, she'd be dead right now. We're getting ready to LifeFlight her out."

Caleb nodded. "Head out. Patrol will clear the way." He watched in sorrow as they rushed out with the stretcher with Darcy lying so still and white. "Where's Doug?"

"I don't know. I kept it off the air until we can find him."

Caleb nodded. "I'll need your weapon, Frankie, just as a matter of course. Someone will be along to get your statement. Head out when you're done." Caleb sighed. "This is not how it was to end, you know."

Frankie shook his head. "No, it wasn't, but God's plans supersede ours. Go find Doug." Frankie's gaze drifted past Caleb. "I'll be heading over to the trauma centre when I'm finished. Did you find the other two?"

Caleb nodded. "We did and have arrested them. Beckett was in town to help. Whitson's mother was here to stop Watson."

Chapter 28

Doug turned as Tom touched his shoulder. Eddie and Caleb were walking towards him, almost in a reluctant manner he thought. Catching the look on their faces, his heart sank. He got her, didn't he, Lord? She's dead.

"Doug." Caleb stopped, a grim white look on his face.

"Tell me, Caleb, is she alive?"

"She is, but she's critical." Tom caught Doug's arm to keep him upright. "The paramedics are on the way to the trauma centre with her. Matt was there and he kept her alive."

"Watson?" Doug's next question was barely audible.

"Someone got him. Frankie didn't get him in time. Come on, we've made arrangements to get you to the trauma centre. There's a chopper waiting for you at the high school. Eddie's going with you. I've sent someone for your mother. They'll make sure she gets there."

Doug nodded, feeling like he was moving in slow motion. Eddie walked beside him as he slowly walked away from the area. He couldn't begin to comprehend how Doug would feel at this point.

Caleb watched as his friend walked away, sorrow clutching at him. Please, Lord, let her live. But Your will be done.

"Where are we at, Tom?"

"Just wrapping it up, Caleb. Just wrapping it up. I'll finish up, debrief the men, and send them home. Our team's not on call overnight and tomorrow. I'll be heading for the trauma centre."

"A lot of our people will be. Frankie said Ian was hit but his vest protected him. Knocked him down and out. He's angry that he couldn't protect her. Matt, I'm not sure how he's feeling."

Tom nodded. "Was it all worthwhile for him? What did he gain?"

"Nothing, Tom, absolutely nothing, and he threw away a career for nothing." Caleb walked away to pace through his town, battered, bruised, but alive. He raised his eyes to the heavens and offered a prayer of thanks, then a prayer for the physicians treating Darcy.

Abe stood beside Ian in the Emergency Room. "How's the back?"

"It's fine. Bruised. Have you heard from Matt?"

Abe shook his head. "No. When you're ready, I'm heading for the trauma centre. Coming?"

"Absolutely. This is the first time we've ever had anyone hurt like this on our watch. I don't like."

"Didn't think you would. When you're ready, the rest of the guys are waiting."

Ian was off the bed and buttoning his shirt, shoving Abe out the door. "Let's get moving. I want to find out how both of them are."

Doug sat in the waiting room, head back, eyes closed. Eddie had made him get his arm looked at. Flesh wound, he thought. I get a flesh wound, and the love of my life is fighting for her life. That's somehow not how I planned today, Lord. It was supposed to be me, not her.

He looked up as Dave sat down beside him and handed him a cup of coffee, coffee that he didn't really want, but took just to keep his hands busy. Dave just sat with his friend, not saying anything, just sitting with him.

Dave looked up and around the waiting room. It was full of Doug's fellow officers and friends. He knew Doug's mother was on her way in. He looked toward the door where he could see Abe's men standing, relaxed but alert. Matt, he hadn't seen, but he had heard from the paramedics who had brought Darcy in that he had gone to the operating room with her, still keeping pressure on the wound.

Abe made his way through the men and women in the room, finally reaching the empty chair on the other side of Doug. He sat.

"Any word yet, Doug?"

Doug looked up, eyes blurry with tears. He shook his head. "Not for a while. A nurse was out just as they were taking her to the operating room. She didn't say much other that she was alive and they would be operating on her. It's been a long time since then."

Abe caught Dave's eyes over Doug's head and the shake of his head. His heart sinking, he knew it would take a miracle for Darcy to survive. He also knew their pastor had started up the prayer chain.

He rose as Doug's mother walked towards him. She touched Doug's shoulder, then cradled her son in her arms. Tears flowed down her face as he wept. The men and women in the waiting room looked, then looked away, uncomfortable with Doug's tears, but knowing they were needed.

Caleb found Eddie somehow in the mass of people and motioned for him to leave. They stepped outside, breathing in the fresh night air, and looking at the stars sparkling in the night sky.

"When I look at a sky like this, I feel so small, Caleb." Eddie's voice was quiet.

"I know how you feel. I stand in awe that a God who created all this and is so amazing could stoop to love even me."

Caleb was silent, thoughts pouring through his mind. Finally, he spoke, "How's Doug?"

"Hanging on by a thread, I would say. He's praying for the best but expecting the worst. Having his mother here helps. No matter how old you get, you always need your parents." He was silent. "We haven't heard anything now for a couple of hours. Matt got word to me that it didn't look good."

Caleb was silent as he absorbed the thought and what it would mean. "No matter which way it goes, it will hurt someone. Our people are hurting. Our town's hurting. The surrounding towns are hurting. No one ever expected a veteran police officer to have been the cause of all this."

"Did the investigators find out anything when they went through his place?"

"They found lots of documents and notes and plans. They'll have weeks of work trying to sort it all out. Whitson has been hospitalized. Apparently he collapsed in his cell. The doctors are looking at a brain tumour and don't think he'll ever stand trial."

"No justice is there?" Eddie turned as Frankie approached them. "Frankie?"

He nodded at them. "Any word?"

They shook their heads.

"We're still waiting. No one's been out of the operating room for a while with an update." Caleb turned as Abe approached. "Abe, I don't like the look on your face."

"No word yet, Caleb. I just needed some air."

Doug looked up as a nurse approached him and then stood. "How is she?"

"She's alive, Lieutenant. The surgeon asked that I come tell you they're still working on her. He thinks it'll be at least another hour or so. It's time consuming for them and for you. They're needing to track down where all the bleeding is coming from and deal with that. They want to do that and find it all without having to take her back in."

"Thank you for coming out, nurse."

She looked at him with compassion and then turned at walked away. Ian watched her face when she turned away from Doug. She really didn't expect Darcy to come out of the operation alive, he could tell. He turned and shoving his way past the men standing around him, walked out of the room and into the night. He walked away from where Abe stood with the other two.

"Ian?"   Murphy's voice sounded behind him.

"Yeah, Murphy?"

"Want to talk?"   Murphy's steps matched his.

"What's to talk about?"

"Ian, you know better than that."

Ian's steps stopped and he nodded. "I'm sorry, Murphy. You're right. I just wish I could have done something to prevent this. And I couldn't."

"No, you couldn't. He got the drop on you somehow. We'll never likely know how he got in."   Murphy looked up as Abe stopped behind them. "Kick yourself all you want, but the decision to help was taken out of your hands. God works in ways we don't understand, Ian, and you're the one who's always telling us that."

Ian nodded, then turned, seeing Abe for the first time, and Caleb and Eddie behind him. "A nurse was out. She says at least another hour. I saw her face. She doesn't think Darcy will make it out of there."

"God knows, Ian. She's not done her work here on earth yet. She'll make it." Eddie turned after he spoke, and headed back for the door.

"Has anybody reached her family?" Murphy asked.

Caleb turned from watching Eddie walk away. "They want nothing to do with her, her parents or her brother and sister. When I called a while ago, her father said she got what she deserved and hung up on me. Darcy had said that they won't talk to her, had in fact moved far away from her. I can't fathom families being like that."

"Nor can I." Abe turned back to the hospital. "I'm heading back in. Maybe there's more word."

Chapter 29

The waiting room had thinned of people. Doug's mother had stretched out on one of the couches, blanket and pillow found for her. He scanned the room out of habit, noting his fellow officers who remained, then his friends and relatives as they stood or sat around, there in support of him.

Doug rose and stretched, needing to move. A twinge in his arm reminded him of his injury, minor he thought when he considered what Darcy was facing. Caleb had talked to him about the investigation. There was still a lot of work to be done now, he knew, and there would be questions that would never be answered. As he neared the door to the operating suite, it opened and the surgeon came out. Seeing Doug, he motioned him back into the waiting room and sat with him.

"How is she, Doctor?"

The surgeon studied him. "She's alive. She shouldn't be, by any means. She should have died back there in her store. She should never have made it here or made it through the surgery." He looked around the waiting room. "You've had people praying, haven't you?"

Doug nodded. "We're a people of faith, Doctor. There have likely been hundreds praying for her and for you and your team."

The surgeon's eyes shot back to Doug, studied him and then nodded. "We could feel them. Just when we would be ready to give up, not able to stop the bleeding, we would find where it was bleeding and be able to stop it. I can't tell you how many times that happened. That young man, Matt, he saved her life, keeping pressure on it right away. Are you going to tell me it was your God that had him there today?"

"He wasn't supposed to be the one with her today. It was to be one of the other men, but Abe put him there instead. So, yes, God worked that out, putting him where he was needed the most."

"That young man has healing in his hands. I understand he works for a security team. That's a waste. He should be out there saving lives."

Doug shook his head. "He's where he's supposed to be. Now, about Darcy?"

"Your fiancee, I understand. She's one lucky lady, Lieutenant. As I said she should be dead. It took a lot to get the bleeding stopped. A couple of times, I thought we were losing her but she rallied. She's in recovery right now, will be there for a couple of hours, and then to an ICU bed. We'll come get you once we've got her moved to ICU. Go, get yourself something to eat. If you have any questions, ask to have me paged. I'll come talk with you." He stood, looking down at Doug. "You've almost convinced me on this God thing."

Doug smiled. "Almost? By the time Darcy leaves, you'll be totally convinced."

The surgeon shook his head as he walked away, Doug's prayers following him. Doug leaned his head back against the wall, fatigue hitting hard. His eyes closed and he slept.

Abe stood and watched his cousin. The news must have been better than earlier. Doug would not sleep if Darcy's life still hung that much in the balance. He turned and walked away, looking for the chapel. He needed to spend time with his God.

Caleb sank into a chair across from Doug and watched. Doug was asleep, either from exhaustion or relief. Caleb's eyes burned with tiredness, but he refused to leave until he talked with Doug. He had talked with Hannah earlier and she assured him that her prayers with them.

Doug started, head coming forward and eyes flying open, then closing again as he realized where he was.

"Doug?" Caleb spoke, startling Doug.

"Caleb. I didn't see you there. Have you been sitting there long?"

"No. Come on, the cafeteria's still open. If you won't eat anything, at least come with me for a coffee for you and a tea for me."

Doug stood, weariness evident in every movement. Seated at a table, Doug looked at Caleb.

"What's on your mind, Caleb?"

Caleb shook his head. "Nothing right now, Doug, other than concern for a friend. Have you had word?"

Doug nodded. "I spoke to the surgeon about an hour ago. She's in recovery and they'll be moving her to ICU soon. Why, Caleb, why her?"

Caleb stared at him. "We're working through that, but Matt did finally get to talk to me. He's giving a statement, but Watson blamed Darcy for keeping Whitson from that group. Somehow, it all warped to include emergency services all over the area. There're many documents we'll need to work through. Doug, Matt did say he thought Darcy had made the decision not to let Watson get to anyone else."

"She would."

Caleb spoke again. "We did catch the one who shot Watson. It wasn't Frankie. It was Beckett's son, Will, in repayment for the lives Watson ruined."

Doug went to speak but stopped when he saw a nurse approaching them.

"Lieutenant Foster, the surgeon wanted me to come get you and take you to your fiancee. We have her settled in ICU now."

Doug rose, then laid a hand on Caleb's shoulder. "Thank you, Caleb."

Doug stood beside Darcy's bedside, first studying the medical equipment he could see but didn't know the names for. He traced the lines running to her arms, IV and blood transfusion. Then, his eyes dropped to her face. A ventilator was in place, breathing for her. He reached a shaky hand, touching her hair and then her cheek. Tears flowed down his face, without his knowing that.

The nurses working around Darcy looked and looked away. They were used to dealing with life and death but this somehow was different. They had heard the story of what had happened and were all amazed she had survived. They walked a little bit more softly around her, feeling like they were in the presence of God.

Doug reached for Darcy's hand and clasped it lightly. He just stood, drinking in the fact that she was still there. God had protected her, not in the way he had asked or expected but He had kept her alive. His heart ached for his lady, knowing she still had a long struggle ahead of her.

He turned at a touch on his shoulder. The surgeon stood there, then motioned for Doug to follow him from the room. Doug turned back to Darcy, bent and dropped a kiss on her forehead and followed the surgeon.

"What is it, Doctor?"

The surgeon's keen but tired eyes studied Doug, noting the exhaustion but the peace he saw. "I just wanted to update you. She's doing better than I expected. If she continues as she is, we'll keep her in ICU for a few days and then move her to a ward. The ventilator is temporary."

Doug nodded. "You're still surprised she's here, aren't you?"

"To tell you the truth, I am. She shouldn't be, you know."

Doug smiled. "I know, but God has a purpose yet for her. She doesn't die unless He says it's her time."

A day later, Doug stood once again at Darcy's bedside. She was starting to move on her own. Her eyes flickered and she blinked, trying to focus. Her eyes found his and he saw the surprise, then joy in hers. His fingers tightened on hers.

"You're in ICU, Darcy. Yes, you're still alive. God protected you."

She gave a small nod and her eyes drifted close again. Thank you, Lord, Doug breathed. Thank you for that sign.

Chapter 30

Two weeks later, Darcy held onto Doug's hands as she gingerly lowered herself to her couch. It was good to be home, but she was still so sore and needed to take time to recuperate. Doug sank down onto the coffee table in front of her, eyes watchful.

"Can I get you anything?" he asked.

She shook her head. Reaching for his hand, she tugged him towards her. "I just need you to hold me for a bit."

He moved to sit beside her, arms around her, gentle in his hold. She rested her head back on him.

"Talk to me, Doug. You've not talked about what happened."

"I know. I just don't know what to say."

"Have you talked to anyone at all or are you just bottling it up inside?"

He smiled. "Still the psychologist, aren't you? Yes, doctor, I did. I talked to our department shrink and then I've been meeting with Greg Evans, our pastor."

"Good. I was worried you hadn't talked to anyone. You can be very quiet when you're working through things. You do love to tease and torment."

A chuckle rumbled through Doug at that. "Tease and torment?"

"Yes. I've been hearing stories about you."

"Me? Must be someone else."

She turned slightly, careful in her movements. "How are your men? And the others in the department?"

"They're hurting, feeling betrayed, but thankful. Caleb's going out of his way to help. Mac's helped as well, free dinners, lunches. He's catered for those working. Our prayer chain has certainly worked over time on this."

"What about the other services and the other towns?"

"The same, but they're working through it. Good support has moved in for each town and service."

She nodded, then grew thoughtful. "How's Ian? I know he blames himself."

"He does but he knows he was ambushed and couldn't help. Matt, now he I was worried about for a while. He took it hard, seeing you go down. He wasn't supposed to be there that day. Abe was sending Murphy, then switched at the last moment."

"God knew who was needed there." She was silent. "I was so worried it would be you."

"I know. When Caleb came to find me, I thought you were dead, just the look on his face. Did I ever tell you about the conversations I had with your surgeon? I wouldn't be surprised to see him at our church one day."

"Oh that would be wonderful. He used to look at me as if I was some kind of miracle or something. Now, let's put that behind us."

Doug's arms tightened around her and he dropped a kiss on her hair. "Let's do that. What do you want to talk about, or do we even need to talk?"

"I think we've talked so much the last few weeks, we've about covered every topic we can think of. Maybe that's why, Doug, this had to happen. Or maybe it was to reach the medical staff." She turned her head to look up at him. "Where do we go from here?"

Eyes fixed in the distance, Doug didn't speak for a few minutes. Then his gaze dropped to hers. "Well, we could talk about the weather or perhaps what you want to do with your store. Abby's certainly taken over there. She loves it and the customers love her. But that's not what's on my mind."

Darcy watched him, silent, a slight smile on her lips.

He smiled. "You're not going to make this easy, are you?" He laughed at her slight negative head movement. "Okay, then here goes. Darcy, we have agreed that we would spend our lives together. Having gone through what we just did, I don't want to wait a long time. When you're healed, will it be enough time to arrange a wedding by then?"

She laughed, then pointed at a spiral-bound notebook on her coffee table. "It's already planned, Doug. Those ladies of Abe's men and your cousin, Rebecca, and Rachel, have helped me plan it. They said it was to take my mind off the healing process. It almost put me back in ICU, laughing so much. They're quite a group."

"So that's why the nurses told me to calm you down." He laughed. "And did you decide a date yet?"

She shook her head. "That's dependent on how well I heal. The surgeon thinks another four weeks, maybe. I guess it was pretty extensive."

"It was. I doubt he told you, but he thought they were losing you a couple of times, and that it was only Matt's keeping pressure on the wound that got you to the hospital. I told him it was God."

"That is was." She hesitated. "Doug, does anyone blame me?"

He stared at her, caught her meaning, and shook his head. "No. Some did at first until the facts came out. The media tried to play it that way, but Caleb pre-empted them with a statement, and they had to eat their words."

"Where was he years ago? I could have used his PR team."

"He was where he was supposed to be. Remember, God's plans are not our plans. What's this I hear from Ian about what you call me?"

"What, my lion?" She laughed at his look. "Ian obviously didn't tell you all that I said. I also said you had the heart of lion, that you protected your family and friends."

He hugged her tighter at then, then sought her lips. He pulled back to look down at her. "Thank you. May you always think that."

He looked around her home. "Now that you're not as busy at the store, any plans?"

"I've always wanted to work on my master's. I was looking for a topic for my thesis."

"Something tells me you found it."

"I have. I've been talking with my new friends, getting their ideas and feelings on why they felt they had to run when they were in danger. It makes a fascinating study. That's my thesis."

Doug started to laugh. "Only you, Darcy, could take a sentence said to you in passing and in fun, and turn it into a thesis. Where will you lead us in the future?"

"Not me, Doug. You. You're the lion in the family, remember?"

Their laughter sounded through the room. They had been apart for years but God had brought them back together and stronger than they would have been. God's plans and purposes had come to fruition in their lives, and they would pass on to future generations that strong faith that had gotten them through the past danger.

Epilogue

Six weeks later, Ian watched as Darcy paced in the small room at the church. Nerves, he thought.

"You're going to wear a hole in the floor, Darcy."

She smiled and kept walking.

"Doug's not running, but if you've talked to all the ladies and have refined how they did it, I can help you run. They'd never find you."

Darcy spun, mouth open, her long white lace-covered dress rustling softly. She went to speak, caught the spark of mischief in Ian's eyes, and shook her head.

"Not this time, Ian. Not this girl. My decision's made and he's waiting out there for me."

"You two make a great couple. Caleb said months ago you were a cute couple, or so I'm told."

She shook her head at him. "Thank you, Ian. You've helped to relieve the nerves. That was your intent all along."

Ian inclined his head, a smile in place. Darcy had asked him to walk her down the aisle and he had been honoured to do so. Her own family still shunned her, and she had been at a loss as to what to do, until she had looked up one day and saw Ian watching her.

A tap at the door, and Dave, one of the ushers, opened it. He nodded when he saw Darcy.

"You look beautiful, Darcy. Doug doesn't stand a chance."

She started laughing at him. "You two. I'll not make it down the aisle without laughing if you keep it up."

"They're ready for you, Darcy."

She tucked her hand into Ian's arm and moved forward, forward towards Doug, the man she loved more than anyone else. Doug turned, overcome by her beauty, then extended his hand to hers.

They had had a rough few months, no years, he thought, but God had brought them back together, stronger in their faith and love for God, and stronger in their love for one another. They were ready to start their new life. No, Doug thought, make that an adventure.

Dear Readers:

Thank you picking up the story of Doug and his lady, Darcy. This was written on the challenge of a friend, Jean West, who told me I should take part in Nanowrimo, National Novel Writer's Month, where the challenge is to write a 50,000 word novel in a month. I must admit, with the words flowing, it didn't take that long.

The premise of this book is that God has a plan and purpose for each of us. With Doug and Darcy, they separated after college, each going their own way. God had a purpose in that, as is shown throughout the book.

What is God's plan for your life? Are you open to His leading, even if it takes you down paths you would never think to go? I've been down some of those paths, knowing God was in control and He alone knows the outcome.

As you travel through your life, keep your eyes fastened firmly on Him. Wait for His plans and purposes, knowing that sometimes we never know why or how until we reach heaven. My father always maintained that if you were delayed somehow in your journey, that God was in that, preventing something we never knew would happen.

Thank you, once again, Faye Silvestro Kubassek, dear friend and sister in Christ, for taking time to proofread, critique, and keep me covered in prayer.

God bless each one of you.

Ronna